A
HAUNTING
IN
HIALEAH
GARDENS

A
HAUNTING
IN
HIALEAH
GARDENS

A NOVEL

RAUL PALMA

DUTTON

DUTTON

An imprint of Penguin Random House LLC
penguinrandomhouse.com

LIBRARY OF CONGRESS CATALOGING-IN-PUBLICATION DATA
Names: Palma, Raul, author.
Title: A haunting in Hialeah Gardens : a novel / Raul Palma.
Description: New York : Dutton, [2023]
Identifiers: LCCN 2023019401 | ISBN 9780593472118
(hardcover) | ISBN 9780593472125 (ebook)
Subjects: LCGFT: Novels.
Classification: LCC PS3616.A33877 H38 2023 | DDC 813/.6—dc23/eng/20230505
LC record available at https://lccn.loc.gov/2023019401

Printed in the United States of America

1st Printing

Interior art: Floral background © Alenarbuz / Shutterstock

BOOK DESIGN BY ALISON CNOCKAERT

For my wife, Mix

A
HAUNTING
IN
HIALEAH
GARDENS

PART I

HUGO
AND HIS DEBTS

1

IT WAS CHRISTMASTIME in Miami, and Hugo hadn't been sleeping well because every time he tried, he'd feel his indebtedness drop into bed with him, this invisible thing. Sometimes it would take hold of his hand, kiss him, then wrap itself around his chest so that it hurt to breathe, or it would slap him awake and demand attention. It was impossible to sleep. It was impossible to imagine a future.

He lived in an efficiency. When he sat at his table drinking tea, he could hear the murmur of another family through the drywall. The children whined, laughed, dribbled basketballs. Their noises made him feel like he lived in a *real* home. From his window, he'd watch them—all in school uniforms—march across the street at 7:05 a.m. to catch the school bus. He'd wanted to be a father.

But Meli was dead, and even if she were still alive and he'd managed to be a better husband, they'd always been broke and in want of what they could not afford. They used to browse retail catalogues in the golden hours of the afternoon, but now Hugo tossed them directly in the trash. He avoided her favorite fast-food restaurants and instead practiced growing romaine lettuce on his windowsill. He had no desire for new romantic partners. He barely had the will to eat.

His only splurge: On Fridays, he'd drive to La Carreta and order a $2.25 café con leche. He kept a quarter on him for a tip. This one extravagant outing amounted to $10 per month, and though it pained Hugo to overpay for coffee, he needed the company of others. More than the coffee, making a transaction with Barbara, the eldest of the cafeteria workers, brought him dignity.

Perhaps it was because she always had nice things to say about his appearance—the clean linen of his tunic, his ceremonial orisha hat, his beaded amulets. When Barbara would reach out and hold his hand, Hugo would pretend he was a true priest, like Lourdes, his supervisor at the Miami Botanica & Spa in Hialeah. He pretended because he was an imposter. He knew this, yet his work depended on him acting as if he were ordained and capable of giving the divination that is received in Ifa.

Sometimes, while enjoying a cafecito at the window, he'd hear other patrons take note of him—neither Cuban nor Afro-Cuban nor Caribbean. Hugo looked Quechuan or mestizo. You'd think, in a city like Miami, the larger Cuban American population would be used to seeing more Indigenous-looking South Americans, but it did not feel that way. He tried not to pay attention.

It being just days before Christmas, he'd gone to the window to give Barbarita a little gift—a devotional from his place of employment. He knew the present was nothing extraordinary, but he'd wrapped it using the remainder of the gift paper he'd found tucked away in Meli's closet. It was nice paper, blue with white snowflakes, and even though Meli used to do all the wrapping, he did well wrapping it on his own. At the counter, Barbara greeted him with her customary "¿Qué me dice?" She slid his coffee over. "Do my eyes deceive me? Hugo. It's not Friday! Got your days scrambled?"

"I wanted to surprise you," he said, and he blushed feeling all the warmth of the season inside him. And Barbara, in her response, squeezed his hand with a strength he did not know that she had. Suddenly, his phone buzzed and rang, startling him badly. Hugo excused himself and studied the unknown number. It seemed familiar, and he wondered, *Should I answer it or let it go to voicemail?*, and feeling a sense of optimism, he answered, "Yes. Hello."

"Is this Hugo Contreras?"

He'd heard the man's voice before, but he did not know where.

"Hello? Hello?" the voice probed. "Can you hear me?"

"Who is this?"

"Alexi Ramirez." Hearing *that* name uttered by *that* man sent Hugo way back—to him and Meli curled under the bare down duvet insert of their bed, the murmur of Ramirez's late-night commercials carrying them off to sleep, A/C blasting. How Hugo missed those quiet nights.

"Is it really you?" Hugo asked. "The attorney on the bus benches?"

When the voice chuckled and responded, "Wow! Yes. That *was* me. A long time ago," Hugo took Barbara's gift and walked off, even though he hadn't sipped his coffee or paid. He paced the lot,

5

weaving in and out of parked cars; then he paused and whispered into his phone, "Do you know who I am, you son of a bitch?" Before Alexi could respond, Hugo raised his voice and said, "You need to stop calling me! What do I got to do to get your people to stop fucking calling me?"

"Hugo . . ."

"It's every day. Every fucking day. And you hide your number on caller ID. Isn't spoofing your number illegal? Tell me, Alexi. Should I file a complaint with the Federal Trade Commission?" He yelled all of this, even with police officers nearby. Hugo's indebtedness, which had been trying to latch onto him all day, slunk to the ground and pooled around his feet. Hugo stomped through it, kicking it so that it felt, for a moment, as if he'd actually conquered his debts once and for all.

Alexi didn't hang up. He waited for Hugo to stop yelling; then he delicately explained why he'd called: "Look. I get it. I'm a debt collection attorney. But I'm being haunted. And it's not just me. I have a wife, a daughter. There's more to me than the work I do. Can you please help me?"

Hugo sat in his car considering the attorney's plea. He pitied him. But even with his indebtedness festering and crawling on his skin like worms, he said, "I'm sorry. I won't help you."

IN MIAMI-DADE COUNTY, most people remember Alexi as the traffic-ticket attorney on the bus-bench ads. He was something unfortunate to stare at during the monotony of rush hour. The ad was so dramatic, like a bad yearbook photo: Alexi, fat, bald, posing with his clenched fist under his chin—an angry American bald eagle squawking behind him. It was the kind of face that made you want to stop your car and doodle something all over it. Whenever Meli would notice one of the ads, she'd close her fist and press it against her chin and say, "No pagues ese *ticket*." What could Hugo say? When she got a ticket going fifteen over the limit, he knew whom to call without even consulting the Yellow Pages. Alexi's firm got her off with a small fine and no points. And there was even something about the jingle (*No points, no points, Ramirez. No points. No points, zoom zoom.*)—Meli would sing the tune without realizing she was doing it. This is to say, Alexi was in the background of their life, creeping in, but they barely paid attention to him.

It took Hugo and Meli quite some time to notice when, in 2015, the bus-bench ads began to bleach in the sun. Those that remained were in bad shape, hardly recognizable and marked up with mustaches and penises. Meli noticed first. "Mira, Hugo. The ads are leaving us. Where's our friend going?" She was so shocked that she called Alexi's ticket clinic while sitting in traffic. She put her phone on speaker so that Hugo could hear the "We're sorry. You have reached a number that has been disconnected or is no longer in service." "No, I don't believe it," she said. "We need to find him, bro."

"Ask Siri."

"No!" Meli said. "Who cares about him! We need to find a bench with his pudgy little face."

In rush hour, they searched the streets. It was nonsensical. Something about finding Alexi had infected them, much in the way that searching for a lost set of keys can drive a person mad.

It was clear to Hugo that finding Alexi's face meant something more to Meli, and though he grew tired and hungry and annoyed by the desperation of commuters, he persisted until they did find one of his ads, completely intact. No mustaches. No penises. Just a piece of gum on Alexi's nose, which she easily scraped off with her fingernail. Meli said, "How do you think he'd look with hair?" Then, using a red Sharpie she kept on her for tagging up commonplace signage, she conjured up a trendy little hairdo, all spiked up in the front like Ricky Martin's. It was ridiculous, yet it brought Hugo and Meli such joy. Afterward, they said their goodbyes to bus-bench Alexi and, for years, forgot him.

Until the phone calls started.

They'd be out, usually at Islas Canarias eating Cuban food, when Hugo's phone would go off, always so damn loud. In those situations, he'd pretend that he didn't hear the ringing, that he didn't see his phone vibrating off the table, that he wasn't aware of the patrons staring, wondering, *Why doesn't he just answer it?* He'd cut into his steak and continue his conversation with Meli, and she learned not to ask who was calling. She tried to teach him how to silence his phone, but even that unsettled him. She'd asked, once, "So how many girlfriends you got, anyways?" And she laughed real good, though Hugo could see that she meant it. "Don't say things like that," he said. "Not ever."

Back then, Hugo's indebtedness was like a mosquito splattered on his car's windshield. It annoyed him, but only mildly. It was easy to ignore. It had only taken a little blood. Hugo knew about the statute of limitations. He knew there was no reason to pay the $2,000 he'd defaulted on during his twenties. He knew that the original creditor had, long ago, sold the debt to a third party;

the creditor had written off the loss to reduce the tax burden on profits from other accounts. It wasn't like he'd taken money from someone. He'd taken it from a corporation that had anticipated, in its business plan, that some debtors would default. This is to say, Hugo had zero remorse. As far as he was concerned, he'd always been in debt. He was indebted to God the day he was born. Carrying such debt, in his mind, was like forgetting that you are also made of flesh and bone.

But he hated the phone calls. He hated how invasive they were and what they implied. Meli would pretend not to notice, and Hugo hated that he was putting her in that situation in the first place. That one time she'd taken his phone to put it on silent mode, he'd seized it back and said, in public, "Don't touch," with such a force that Meli looked as if he'd slapped her. His words made her cry. How he wanted to simply be free of his past blunders—to be an unbaptized child, forgotten by God and devil and belonging only to himself—which was why, one night, after he'd looked at his savings account, he answered one of those unwanted calls. It was bold. He was in bed with Meli, watching reruns of *Mr. Bean* and eating popcorn, and he blurted out, "Won't. You. Stop calling?"

The way he said it, with no warmth, really startled Meli.

On the line, a prerecorded message noted that the phone call was an attempt to collect a debt. It was a message on repeat, vocalized by someone for whom English was not their dominant language. There was something menacing about the recording, the way it'd repeat, all staticky and silvery, as if it were just some transcript reverberating endlessly in some metallic void. The recording reminded him of the complex and frayed speakers within

the mine he'd once worked in—a lifetime ago as a young child—
and how the supervisor would announce lunch breaks and shift
changes, always in a voice that was distorted and far-off-seeming.
Hugo could almost see the sadness of his brother's face, soft under
the glow of the many oil-lit lanterns. He didn't want to go back
there.

When the debt collector finally came to the line, Hugo said,
"Come on! It's Sunday night."

The young woman on the line asked, "Am I speaking with—"

"You know that it's me."

Meli pulled at the sheets. From beneath the nest of the duvet
insert and the unfolded laundry, she kicked him off the bed with
her bare foot and whispered, "Go get me some Diet Coke."

Hugo took the call to the kitchen.

"I'm calling regarding your Bank of America credit card debt."

"I know. I know. Can't I just pay it right now, over the phone?"

"Yes! Great! I can walk you through the payment options—"

"I just want to pay."

"But sir—"

"Are you going to take my checking info or what?"

"Of course, Mr. Contreras. How much would you like to pay?"

Hugo told her that he'd pay the $2,000. He gave her his checking
information, and he asked her to mail him a receipt. That night,
he jumped back into bed with Meli, and he felt liberated, exorcised
of his past financial missteps, even if he'd blown through half of
his savings. He kissed her, climbed between her legs, and told her
what he'd done as if he'd conquered a mountain—as if the many
peaks and walls and barriers surrounding him had fallen away to
some celestial halo.

"That was so stupid," Meli said. "We could have gone to Disney!"

"Disney?"

"And you forgot my Diet Coke," she said, kicking him off the bed again. "Please!"

For Hugo, making the payment was absolutely worth it—even if Meli didn't see it that way—until he received his receipt in the mail. It showed that he still owed $14,476. The law firm had calculated sixteen years of high interest. He called, disputing the amount and refusing to pay, always prompted to listen to that recorded message, but in the end there was no escaping the total debt.

What the firm did was a crime. Yet *they* sent him to court, and the judge ruled in *their* favor. The statute of limitations had reset when he'd made a payment. He'd opened his door wide open and invited that attorney right in. By the end of the year, Hugo's wages were being garnished. The little he made at the botanica was less, so he relied on credit cards for groceries and gas. With the high interest, Hugo knew that he'd never pay off his debt, and it angered him—how the missteps he'd made could haunt him forever. He didn't want to talk about it. Meli wished that he would.

Maybe Hugo could have forgiven Alexi for that mess, but six years after Hugo's $2,000 payment, Alexi came for them all over again. Hugo's credit cards were maxed out, and Meli was gone, and there was still Diet Coke in the fridge, unopened, and the phone calls were becoming incessant, this time for another kind of debt. Hugo had, without fully realizing it, cosigned on Meli's hospital bills. He could only vaguely remember having done so. Through the wake and the funeral, he ignored the calls, but between the phone ringing and Meli's aunt Lena shoving him and saying, "Have you no respect?" and the priest reading the rites and giving Hugo the side-eye, there was no peace. On the road nearby, a dozen or so motorcycles revved their engines. Overhead, a traffic helicopter hovered. It was so ordinary. And maybe there was something else preventing him from grieving her loss. In remembering Meli, he could only recall another person. The thought was parasitic.

Worse, after the burial, nobody left him alone. Even Lena, who'd never cared for him to begin with, insisted on having lunch. She took his hand and said, "She still lives with us, you know?"

Hugo shuddered at the touch and said, "No, she doesn't. Why would you say that? We just buried her." When he left the cemetery on that morning, finally alone, he went home and checked his mailbox, a ritual born of habit, nothing else. Inside the rusted little box, there was a certified letter from the Law Offices of Alexi Ramirez & Associates—the only correspondence that day.

Hugo opened it, and what he saw weren't numbers or figures; he saw just one word, "COLLECT," which seemed in that moment to be an attempt on his soul. That night, he drank to end it all, but he must have not drunk enough. Because he did awaken the next morning, head pounding, and he saw Alexi's court summons, and sitting across from him, where Meli would take her coffee, he saw something else: his indebtedness. It was as hot and as bright as the Florida sun.

IN THE PARKING LOT, Hugo was toying with his rosary, which he wore around his wrist, peeling off strips of leather from its beads. He was getting ready to hang up when Alexi blurted out, "Wait! We can work out a deal. How about this? You help me, and I'll clear your debt like it never even happened. You help me for real, and I'll clear all of it—every penny. Listen! You can be mad at me, but think this through. I mean, if your boss says you are what you are, if you can cleanse my house so that there isn't a spirit left in it, I'll forgive all your debt." Sitting idle in the parking lot, Hugo considered Alexi's proposition. *Can Alexi really do such a thing? What of my emotional debt? And what of my debt to Meli?* Hugo felt his indebtedness, the way it suffocated him at all times, the way it infected every aspect of his life, every free space, every new relationship—an invisible thing that somehow felt opaque and as solid as a bank vault at the bottom of the sea. "Sure. I'll meet you."

2

AFTER LEAVING LA CARRETA, Hugo drove to the botanica, a small shop in a strip mall overflowing with sacred relics—over five thousand spiritual, occult, and religious items, from devotional candles to incense to live fowl. This was no ordinary botanica. Lourdes was the retailer of choice to the many spiritual leaders of Miami. An editor at the *Miami New Times* deemed it the "Ñooo! Que Barato! of Spiritual Goods," a designation that Lourdes displayed proudly on a plaque behind the cash register.

When hurricanes broiled off the coast, threatening the whole of South Florida, reporters would assemble outside her store to await her divinations. And Lourdes, aware of the good publicity, would set up her carved-wood divination tray in the parking lot and ask Elegua, the Eshu, for permission to begin the ritual. She did this by pouring palm oil directly onto the effigy. The oil was red like blood. The first time Hugo saw her perform this ritual, he was horrified. "Cálmate! It's not like we're sacrificing roosters every single day," she said. "But we must feed the orisha something. So palm oil it is." Lourdes then chanted the Odu Ifa verses—centuries-old narratives passed down from one babaláwo to another—while pressing palm nuts. She wore no extravagant outfits. She covered her hair with linen and the lantana flowers that grew in the strip mall, and she knelt over the tray, straining, with a thick unmarked cigar in her mouth, already lit.

If she was the grotto, Hugo was the adjacent gift shop. He'd sit under a canopy selling hurricane-survival packages—devotionals, sage, anything that brought comfort—at $20 a pop. These hurricane-divination events were wildly popular, with long lines that rivaled those at the gas stations, and though it all seemed like "mumbo jumbo," as Hugo liked to say, Lourdes was never wrong.

To the dismay of local building contractors, many of whom lit candles in hopes of a hurricane landfall, Lourdes frequently predicted that storms would veer north. When contractors frustrated by her divination would call her integrity into question, she'd remind everyone that even before Bryan Norcross knew Hurricane Andrew's fate, she predicted the 1992 storm would strike Homestead. It was true. Even when Andrew was forecast to cut through Calle Ocho and Little Havana, her vision of Andrew ripping through Homestead made her a legend in the community.

In 2017, Walter Mercado himself called the botanica to see what Lourdes thought of Hurricane Maria. She put Walter on speaker so that Hugo could hear the famed astrologer's voice. Then she said, "Walter, mi amigo blanquito, I'm surprised by this. Haven't you read the stars?" And she laughed so loud until she grew somber and said, "If even *you* can't see her path, prepárate."

Of course she was right. When Puerto Rico lost electricity, she didn't turn on the store lights, in solidarity.

And people didn't only think of Lourdes in times of existential threat. When those in the community, or even some in the larger Miami diaspora, desired good health and fortune or love, it was Lourdes whom they'd contact. Her botanica could ship goods anywhere in the United States in two days. Her store was like Amazon, except Lourdes didn't have a website, nor did she need one. Those who called often didn't know what they required. It was up to her to find out. And this was how she first trained Hugo: "Listen to them, and the best relics will show themselves to you."

Though Hugo was a nonbeliever, he respected Lourdes, and he followed her instructions without question. When he first started consulting with clients by telephone, he was amazed that her technique did, in fact, work. Sometimes, while listening to someone vent about a colleague or express worry about a child, Hugo would become overwhelmed by his lack of knowledge, but then, in the many racks of the store, he would feel one item calling to him—a kind of vibration. He couldn't explain why or how this happened, but this item, when delivered to the client, would solve the issue.

This was how Hugo came to believe that if any magic existed, it existed in her. Which was why, now, Hugo was upset with Lourdes. Even without divination, Lourdes knew Alexi garnished his wages. She saw it in the payroll. Hugo focused all of his attention on one thought—¡*Vete al carajo!*—hoping that, from his spot in Westchester, she could divine those words in Hialeah, imprinted on a cloud or a puff of smoke, or whatever magical utterance they'd appear to her in.

~

WHEN HUGO EVENTUALLY barged into the botanica sweating and out of breath, Lourdes, who was in the midst of helping a customer, excused herself and embraced him. "Hugo!" she said, and then paused, like she was expecting a "thank you" or some positive reaction. When none came, she said, "Oh! That's right. You want me to go to hell. You're such a bobo." Then she returned to her customer, punctuating her remark by shouting, "He's forgiving your debt. Didn't he tell you?"

Hugo stomped off to the storage room and slammed the door shut. He closed his eyes and, listening to the inventory of chickens cluck in their cages, wondered, *Why did I agree to help this man?*

To begin, Hugo would need some materials. The shelves lacked holy water, so he seized a box cutter and cut open the newly arrived shipments. As he did so, he imagined sitting at one of Alexi's old bus benches and flaying the printed face clean off, leaving nothing but the wood of the backrest. He could feel his indebtedness climbing through his arm like a cramp, urging him to make it so. Such thoughts, when he could rein them in, disgusted him. Only after he'd pocketed a Virgin Mary plastic statue bottle filled with holy water, along with the box cutter itself, did he notice Lourdes observing him. She held him by the shoulders and said, "I know how you despise this man. But you've been carrying this debt too long. You wear it like chains. This can free you, cariño."

"It's not the debt," he said. "It's the man."

"Tú sabes," she said, caressing his arm. "He didn't take Meli from you. God did."

"He didn't take her. Fine. But he put a lien on her. I pay him her debts every month."

"But it is his business," Lourdes said.

"It's the business of devils."

"You're right," Lourdes said, shaking her head. "But devils are our business."

"Why should that man be the one to forgive me?"

"You know, you very well could forgive him? You are a ba-baláwo."

~

ALL SPIRITUAL PEOPLE, Hugo believes, walk upon this globe contending with the fear that they are imposters. Every time Hugo visits with a client, he puts on a grand show, but it's all smoke and mirrors. It's all garments and candles and sacrifices that divert the eye away from his primary mission—fact-finding. All that Hugo does in his role as babaláwo is set the atmosphere; he creates the perfect conditions for confession and revelation. He invokes the fear of God and of Satan in everyday objects. Then he uses that information to manufacture a ritual that fits the situation.

Some years ago, just months after Obama's reelection, Lourdes put Hugo on a rather standard case. An older gentleman named Wilfredo had come into the botanica out of sorts because he believed that his father was trying to kill him—his father who'd died fifty-one years prior while fighting in the Bay of Pigs invasion. The story made no sense to Hugo. More so, during a preliminary meeting, Hugo found it difficult to take Wilfredo seriously—a fit man well into his seventies, balding, and covered with a thick mat of white body hair. He looked like the kind of guy who'd served in the military himself and still maintained a regimen of push-ups at home. He was a serious man, a general contractor who oversaw a fleet of other contractors. Yet there he was, nestled in the back room of the Miami Botanica & Spa in Hialeah, almost in tears over his torments.

"So your father, who is fifty-one years dead, has been trying to kill you?" Hugo asked.

"Yes."

"And how do you know it's him? This spirit?"

"Excuse me," Wilfredo said. "Do you find this funny?"

Hugo could hardly contain himself. "No. No. Please. Answer my question."

"I know it's him because it looks like him."

"But in what state? Is he young? Old? Is he returned from the grave?"

"Young. Old," Wilfredo said. "What difference does it make? Can you help me, or not?"

It took three visits to the client's home to figure out what was going on. During that time, Hugo learned much about Wilfredo. He learned, for example, that the first time he'd realized that his father was trying to kill him was during a lightning storm. Wilfredo had been out picking fallen mangoes from his family home when a single bolt of lightning struck down the tree that he and his father had planted together the spring before his death. One limb, overburdened by fruit, fell right on Wilfredo's shoulder, knocking him out cold. When he awoke, he was soaked and muddy and covered in leaves, and he felt a voice with the warmth of burnt tobacco whisper, "No eres hijo mío."

20

Another time, Wilfredo was fishing under the Rickenbacker Causeway at night when something seized his line and ran. Wilfredo said that he thought it might be a shark or a fucking whale. He reeled it in like his life depended on it, and when he pulled up that opaque mass, what he saw was his own father's face, all mangled and decomposed—an eel slithering out where there'd once been an eye. This frightened Wilfredo so much that he slipped off the ledge and fell into the cold and powerful current. He reached for the shore, but the current was relentless, and in the moment when he thought he might be swept out to sea, he reached for the seafloor and realized that he was, in fact, in shallow water. He could stand. "That was my father," he said. "It was the hand of my father, trying to drag me down to the bottom of the sea. Why does he hate me?"

Hugo was at a loss. Wilfredo's father, in the brief luminous years before the Bay of Pigs, seemed like a good man. "He was amazing," Wilfredo had said. "The best dad, truly!" His father would come home after training in the Everglades to kill Fidel, and in their small fenced-in yard, he'd play a round of Kill the Communists, brandishing sticks as guns, liberating Cuba before dinner.

On Hugo's third visit, it all clicked for him. He noticed something that didn't quite fit the picture. He couldn't believe he hadn't noticed it before. There, on Wilfredo's refrigerator, was a portrait of President Obama with a dedication: "Thank you, Willy, for your support! God bless." It was practically vibrating, much in the way that the objects in Lourdes's botanica would during consults. "What's that?" Hugo asked, sliding the magnet off and holding it. "Did you vote for Obama?"

Wilfredo pushed his seat back and said, "I can vote for who I want."

"Sure. Yeah," Hugo said. "I like him, too, but what would your father say?"

"He'd be furious."

"Why is that?"

At this, Wilfredo seemed to realize what Hugo was insinuating.

"When did the tree get struck by lightning again?" Hugo asked.

"I think it was November."

"November sixth? His reelection?"

"No. But. Coño. It was the day after!"

"Yes. I thought so."

Wilfredo took the picture, gazed at it longingly. "What do I have to do then?"

"Here's what I recommend. Vanquish the photo."

"What?"

"I'll come here tonight, and we'll destroy it."

"You think that will work?" Wilfredo asked.

"Well, it's a start. Listen. I'll come tonight. Anything Obama-related, have it waiting on the back porch. And I mean anything. A pencil. A letter. A T-shirt. Hell, anything Democratic. Got it?"

"And how about Clinton?"

"Bill is okay. But if it's Hillary, maybe toss that, too."

That night, Hugo returned ready. He brought a spiritual bath. He brought a Ziploc bag filled with chicken bones. Together, they marched into Wilfredo's backyard, right beside the fallen mango tree. "After today, no more Obama memorabilia," Hugo said. "After today, take your Democratic affiliation and tear it up. You

don't have to be a Republican, but you're done. Do you understand?"

Wilfredo nodded.

"Should I proceed?"

"I can feel him watching me."

"Feel him?"

Hugo lit the devotionals, tossed the Obama gear in the box,
tossed the chicken bones in, then poured lighter fluid all over it
and set the whole thing ablaze. For theatrics, he'd left a pouch of
barium chloride in the box, which burned green. It must have
looked, to Wilfredo, like Hugo was exorcising the devil himself.
He must have seen, in the smoke and flames, the face of his father
because during the ritual, Wilfredo buckled over in tears and
yelled, "I'm sorry, Papi. I'm sorry."

But what had Hugo actually done? Nothing. Hugo could boil
it down to science. For Hugo, the thought of someone's spirit stay-
ing behind after death was ridiculous. The thought of a soul made
him laugh. How could people believe such a thing in an age of
science and the internet? But watching Wilfredo arrive at an
emotional high, and feeling nothing in return, made Hugo feel
abject.

Reflecting on Wilfredo's situation, Hugo was envious. *How
could it be*, he wondered, *that a stranger could have such a profound
experience with the ghost of a loved one, and I can't even remember
Meli's face?* What he remembered were the things she wanted—all
her incomplete dreams and wishes—the nice house in Coral Ga-
bles with the oak tree, the fancy white BMW, the walk-in closet
with a floor-to-ceiling shoe rack. The list went on. There was so
much. Meli had always felt that, maybe, one day, it would happen.

Her life depended on that idea. But Hugo knew better. The day would never come. He'd always known it. When Meli would blurt out her long lists of wants, or when she'd sit on the couch and circle various pieces of luxury furniture in catalogues, Hugo would feel his impotence burning in him, and when Meli would say, "This year is going to be our year," Hugo would nod along, like he really believed her, and he'd let this lack fester and rot until he resented her dreams.

When she died, and when her aunt Lena had to be the one to buy the coffin, he felt useless—not her husband, not the man she deserved, who would move the world for the love of his life, but just a placeholder. He should have at least paid for the coffin, even if it wasn't made of mahogany.

Remembering Wilfredo burning his possessions in order to mourn his father, Hugo wondered what he could burn of Meli's. The lists she'd made? The things she'd never purchased? Wilfredo's situation, at least, turned out positive. The hauntings stopped. Hugo knew because Wilfredo would visit to replenish the devotionals, convinced that if he ever forgot to light them, the spirit of his Obama-hating father would return to exact revenge. Even with this success, however, Hugo was not convinced that he'd done anything, or that anything supernatural had occurred. As far as Hugo knew, Wilfredo's hauntings could be chalked up to some undigested Sarussi sandwich throwing off his equilibrium. The guilt had been in Wilfredo all along. That's all it'd ever been. Most hauntings worked that way. Someone felt bad about something, and that negativity manifested as a ghost.

3

~~∾⊙⊙∽~~

HUGO'S NAVIGATION APP reported an accident and re-routed him to the Florida Turnpike. Hugo merged into traffic. He was in better spirits. He rarely crossed under the Palmetto Expressway. In his imagination, this tract of Miami-Dade County—of unincorporated communities, many of which were developed on the heels of the subprime mortgage crisis—was bound to offer something nice to look at. He imagined palatial gated communities, the kinds with fountains and geese and perfectly landscaped exteriors. He imagined royal palms and swimming pools and lots of new construction, but as he drove, he saw that he was leaving neighborhoods behind for industry and desolation.

On the Florida Turnpike, he passed one massive warehouse after another, each an exporting company with an empty parking lot. Once on US 27, Hugo was not sure where Hialeah Gardens began and Medley ended. On the map, Hialeah Gardens looked like a crosscut saw. This seemed purposeful—four saw teeth cutting into the greater Miami-Dade, a desperate attempt to delineate the Gardens from Hialeah proper and Miami Lakes to the far north. This was a place, surely, that wanted its own identity, but the zoning baffled him: a stone quarry, various cement suppliers, a meat distributor, all within proximity to new schools, a library, and a park. Hugo had seen a fleet service company and a forklift dealer and a herd of sickly-looking cattle grazing in a piney field. He'd seen abandoned lots with old trailers, the word "office" hand-painted on the walls. A Realtor might describe the city as raw, modern-leaning, industrial chic. But to Hugo, it looked dry and destitute, a nice stronghold for a zombie apocalypse but no place to raise a family if one could avoid doing so.

Alexi Ramirez was out front when Hugo pulled up into the driveway. *I must have written the wrong address*, Hugo thought. *This can't be the place.* It was no "home," that was for sure. "Dwelling" seemed the most suitable word, a place where things nest, an earthy cropping of glass and stone. The mansion reminded Hugo of a zoo—one he had seen as a boy new to this country. He'd arrived in Omaha, where the sky was impossibly vast, and before he saw where he'd be living, he insisted on seeing the animals. He'd never seen so many things captured in one place. At first, the animals looked perfectly at home, in cages that really did resemble their habitats, but then Hugo saw the steel bars, and he snuck glimpses of behind the scenes—the antiseptic chambers where the staff attended to the creatures. He saw the shit stains, the sick animals, and all not intended for the public's view.

Yes. Alexi's house really reminded him of those enclosures, the American dream, all mere concrete and creative landscaping designed to conceal something. Who would know, just looking from the curb, that Alexi's home had been financed through debt, a dollar at a time, extracted from the poorest of the poor through persuasion or judgment. Hugo could admire it, certainly. It was a far cry from his efficiency, but he could not unsee the incessant phone calls, the bills stacked in his mailbox, the machinery of Alexi's debt collection engine pumping in cash from all over the state. In scanning the premises, he wondered, *What has my pain contributed to? The fountain? The potted topiaries?*

Hugo killed the engine, wiped sweat off his brow. He admired the seagulls gyrating in the sky, which made it seem like the Gardens were near an ocean and not the county's largest landfill.

~

ALEXI TAPPED ON the car window with his knuckles. He was dressed in khaki shorts and a linen short-sleeve button-up, which seemed fitting as it was an oppressively humid day, even by South Florida's standards. To be clear, the outfit choice was fitting, but neither Alexi's shirt nor his shorts fit him in the least; they were two sizes too large. He looked like a buffoon. This had been a mistake. Hugo did not want to meet the man. He considered hitting reverse and driving off. He even started the car again and motioned as if to shift into reverse, but Alexi was too close, and Hugo thought he might roll over some of the attorney's toes. "Hi! Everything all right in there?" Alexi knocked again.

Hugo stepped out of the car, wholly unprepared for the foulness of the city dump. "It's the wind," Alexi said. "It usually doesn't blow this way. Your lucky day." With that sarcastic tone, he approached Hugo. Yes. There it was, Alexi's bus-bench face.

How familiar, its roundness and perpetual scowl, and the disgusting scruff of his beard. Hugo almost didn't shake his hand, but the attorney was so forthright, his open palm an invitation, so Hugo played nice. They shook hands vigorously, and Alexi thanked him, warmly, for coming to his aid in spite of everything. "I know this is not ideal," he said. "I'm grateful that you can put so much behind you to help my family."

"It is the season," Hugo said, and Alexi touched his arm and chuckled convulsively. This was meant to be a warm gesture, a friendly welcome, but in that moment Hugo felt at his mercy, a saltshaker at the dinner table. It reminded him of the way his indebtedness would seize his wrist and turn over his forearm, exposing the network of veins and capillaries along his wrist. *Cut. Cut.* And was not every phone call, every letter, every attempt to collect a debt some form of Alexi reaching out, trying to take hold? Hugo felt impotent, poor in the world: a bee with its abdomen removed.

It was especially disorienting for Hugo to understand the man, not just as a face on a bus bench or a name on certified mail, but as a person, quite ordinary, yes, heavy but fragile and in good spirits. Hugo thought he even seemed friendly, this debt collector, living the high life by squeezing dollars from grieving widowers. He was a real devil. Hugo knew that, and maybe that's why Alexi had been able to so easily disarm him. They stood in front of the complex, alongside a giant inflatable Frosty the Snowman and a dozen lawn candy canes, discussing the temperature this time of year. It was the usual *yay, Miami* bullshit: *Aren't we lucky to be down here during the winter? Who could live in the snow?*

Alexi pulled out a checkbook, clicked ready a pen.

Hugo laughed and waved off the gesture.

"Excuse me?"

"It must be bad," Hugo chimed in. "You're willing to cancel my debt?"

"Yes! I'd forgive it. I mean that," he said.

"Then it must be bad," Hugo said, making the sign of the cross.

Alexi nodded. "Sure, but let me ask you something. Lourdes said I'd need a donation?"

"The donation is not for me. It's for the orishas. We are but vessels."

"So, how do I know you won't—"

"Please," Hugo said, cutting him off. "I'd like to get started. May we?"

Alexi hesitated, but then gestured toward the yard and said, "Of course."

Strolling through the Ramirez backyard, it was easy to forget that a single family occupied such an extravagant and expansive home. Even before Hugo saw Alexi's crystalline pool, he heard the gentle rock waterfall, and hearing this made him want to change into a bathing suit and chancletas, and order a mojito. Ghosts. Spirits. Demons. Why was someone so wealthy worrying about such trivial and nonexistent things? Especially when he could be lounging, taking the day off? The patio reminded Hugo of the touristy pool decks out on Miami Beach. It was beautiful, an oasis nestled in Medley's scrap industries, but it was also commercial, designed for the masses, not a hint of personal touch to any of it. Standing by the pool, Hugo felt as though he were trespassing at a hotel, as though security would appear, ask for his room key, and whisk him back to the street.

"That look. You sense something here, don't you?" Alexi asked.

Hugo perked up and, with much effort, ignored the sleek and extravagant furnishings. "Maybe," he said. "Forgive me. You have a beautiful home. Perhaps we can sit to discuss further."

THE TABLE WAS dressed in a rose-colored linen runner. Atop the linen rested a wooden tray, a stove-top cafetera, and two small cups, along with a platter of Manchego cheese and croquetas de jamón. Claudia, Alexi's wife, ran out to meet them. She was in workout clothing, sporting a rose-gold-colored Apple Watch. She pulled out her AirPods when she greeted Hugo. "You're the guy," she said, in between breaths, "who'll chase away the 'bad energy,' right? Good luck." She used air quotes to say "bad energy." Hugo liked her already. "I hope, for my husband's sake, that you can."

"So you don't believe?" Hugo asked.

She laughed. "I'd much sooner believe in butter fairies."

"I don't know these creatures," Hugo said. "What are they?"

"Butter fairies," Claudia said, "sneak into your house at night and—"

"Por favor," Alexi said.

"—wait for it—they steal your butter while you're sleeping."

"No!" Hugo laughed.

"Yes! One little morsel at a time."

"Adorable," Alexi said. "Now. Can you give us a moment?"

Claudia performed some standing stretches, then jogged in place as part of her warm-up. All the while, she maintained eye contact with Hugo. At one point, she stood perfectly erect, shook her arms and legs, then smiled and said, "God! If someone told me that my husband, the great debt collector of Miami, would ever consult with a babaláwo, I wouldn't have believed it. Not ever!"

"Claudia, please," Alexi said.

"God, Alexi! You're just like Gloria, you know? She's rubbing off on you."

"You're being disrespectful."

"It's an insult directed at you. Not our 'esteemed' guest."

"Don't you have somewhere to run off to?" Alexi snapped back.

"See what I have to deal with, babaláwo? You have anything for me? Anything that would make dealing with this man any more bearable? Maybe something to make his sleep apnea go away."

"His time is valuable," Alexi said sternly. "And you are being inappropriate."

"Fine. Promise me this, then. That you'll be done with this nonsense by Noche Buena."

"In three days?" Alexi asked.

"Yes! Three days. We have a party to plan, don't we?"

"I'll discuss that with him."

"Okay, okay. I'll be off then. Please. *Please* keep an ear out for Dulce. You know she gets so caught up in her games," she said, before bounding off through the grass and toward the street.

When Claudia was gone, Alexi apologized. "What can I say?

She is a skeptic." He offered Hugo coffee, and of course Hugo helped himself. Then Alexi asked, "How long have you been in this line of work? I guess I just don't know how someone pursues a career in what you do."

"It's the only job I've had in Miami," Hugo said, which was the truth. What he didn't tell him was that when he graduated from high school, he needed a job, so he walked into every store in a local strip mall to ask if they were hiring. The botanica was the fourth business he visited, and Lourdes hired him on the spot; she claimed that he was destined to do bold and beautiful things. At the time, such a premonition meant nothing to Hugo, but lately he'd been wondering: *What did she see in me?*

Alexi sipped from his coffee. "You probably don't know this about me. I didn't want to be an attorney." He chuckled, broke a croqueta in half. "I wanted to study art history, to travel the world and visit every art museum. But my parents talked some sense into me. Thank God!"

"I'm sorry," Hugo said.

"Sorry! Could you imagine if I'd studied art history? Where would I be now?"

"But it sounds like art is a passion for you. It would make you happy, no?"

"Sure, it's a passion, but it's not a business. You don't make a living off art. Nowadays, too many kids go to college and study the things they're passionate about. It's retarded. You think they ever take a moment to understand how they'll fit into the economy? How they'll pay back their student loans, with their women's and gender studies degrees? Do you think they ever . . . ?"

Hugo didn't want to listen any further. He'd heard conservative Cubans go on these rants before, and it made little sense to have a serious conversation with him. Enjoying a pleasant day by the pool, Hugo could ignore the usual hits: Obama, Trump, "All Lives Matter," liberal wokies.

Still, Hugo did find it quite sad when Alexi revealed that becoming an attorney made his parents proud. "They loved seeing my face on the bus benches," he said. "God bless their souls; they saw my kind of work as an indictment on Castro and communism. In their eyes, I was holding freeloading scoundrels accountable. If I'd studied art history, would I have redeemed their exile? No!" he exclaimed. "I'd be like the Cubans they left behind. Why come to America to be an artist?"

"You have a child, no?" Hugo asked. "Is that the advice you will give to her?"

"Excuse me," he said, gesturing toward his property. "Knowing my family is taken care of is happiness. Knowing that Dulce will be financially secure is happiness. You know what? I had to make a sacrifice, and if I needed to do that so she could follow her passion, great! Then I'm glad."

"Sure."

"Listen, babaláwo. Enough of this. Aren't you supposed to—"

Dulce ran out of the house screaming. She looked like a hot mess, wearing underwear atop her shorts atop a pair of pants. Hugo thought something terrible had happened, the way she yelled. Even Alexi looked concerned, but then she threw herself on her father's lap and laughed, waving her stuffed bear. "Will you say 'hello' to our guest? His name is Hugo," Alexi instructed, handling her.

She ignored him, picking at the bear's eyes instead. She was petite, and there was something pale about her, like a child who didn't get sun or hadn't been eating all that well. "Dulce, listen to your papá when he speaks."

She glanced at Hugo, then buried her head in her father's neck.

Alexi raised his voice, "Dulce! What did I just tell you?"

"To say 'hello.'"

"Well?"

Dulce climbed off him, stood by Hugo, and whispered, "Hello."

"Speak so he can hear you."

"Hello!" she yelled, fists clenched.

"Dulce! With respect."

"Hellll-o," she said, but the way she said it made Hugo feel so bad for her. He wanted to ask if her dad was always like this. So many people in this world witness one injustice after another, and they say nothing. Hugo wanted to say something, but he needed to stay focused. Instead of addressing the obvious tension, Hugo asked, "What's your bear's name? He looks like a Henry."

She smiled, then, clearly bored by the question, ran off. Hugo was struck by the irrational feeling that his indebtedness had run off as well. *Go play*, he thought. *Play. Play.* Yes. In that moment, all of Hugo's demons ran off onto the lawn to play with Dulce. It was nice.

"Are you done with your coffee?"

"She's a cute kid," Hugo said. "What a gift to be her parent."

"Well then," Alexi said. "We should probably get right down to business."

Hugo pushed his coffee aside, set a notepad down on the table. Reaching for his pen, he grabbed the box cutter he'd pocketed. He'd forgotten it was there. A look of alarm must have crossed his face, because Alexi became quite serious: "What is it? Did you just see one of them?"

~

MELI. THE DAY she was laid to rest, she looked all done up, wearing her favorite emerald green Banana Republic dress, which always reminded Hugo of Christmastime. Her hair had been straightened, her eyebrows cleaned up nicely. And because he didn't know what to do with her cell phone, he put it in the coffin right there along with her—not in her hand, but nearby, resting against the fabric liner.

After the burial and the long ride home, all that remained of Meli were her possessions and, as the Law Offices of Alexi Ramirez & Associates was so adept at reminding him, their shared debt.

In the far reaches of his kitchen pantry, he found the cheap bottle of rum that Meli had purchased for some party, and which he had convinced her was not worth the hangover. Through the night, he drank it all. It's not that he wanted to kill himself. At least it didn't begin that way, but while he felt the alcohol overtake him, a strange thought crossed his mind—that maybe Meli wanted him to be dead, too. There was even a moment, in his drunkenness, when he swore he'd heard Meli whisper it. He'd seen her walk into the room, sit by his side, and shove the bottle closer. This was when he decided, enjoying his buzz, that maybe he really *needed* to end things once and for all.

He was disappointed when he awoke the next day feeling like death but still very much alive. He was angry. He had no room in his grief for reason. He wanted to hurt Alexi—to do more than hurt him. Dehydrated and with a throbbing headache, he drove to the law firm with a baseball bat.

With the rising sun refracting against his windshield, he sat through forty-five minutes of traffic on the 836. It was numbing, that commute. All over the city, people were slogging into their cars and drowning in Power 96. He could feel all their grogginess and desperation. *Why do we live like this?*

By the time he inched past Jackson Memorial Hospital, he'd had enough time to sober up and reevaluate his plan. It no longer seemed like such a good decision, but what was he to do? He was already in traffic, and wouldn't it be more work to switch lanes and exit the highway? He didn't want to. He was listening to music and thinking of Meli, so he pressed on and parked in downtown.

Alexi's law firm was located within one of the city's many steel-and-glass skyscrapers. When Hugo crossed the building's monumental and wide-open lobby, already bustling with activity, a young security guard stopped him from accessing the building's elevators. "Señor," he said, putting his hand on Hugo's chest, "where you going with that bat?" The guard looked tired, just like Hugo, and just like everyone in this godforsaken city. He wore his button-up untucked, his tie loose. "Señor, you should go home. Nobody wants trouble here. Believe me," he said. There was something sincere in the young man's voice, which Hugo interpreted as an invitation, so he pleaded his case, belligerently. Then he shouted so that everyone could hear his plan—how he wanted to appeal the law firm's judgment with a swift blow to Alexi's bald head. As all of this was transpiring, with even more guards working to contain Hugo's outburst, Hugo realized that nobody cared. Nobody cared that his wife had died. Nobody cared that Alexi's firm had purchased his wife's medical debt, or that they were profiting from Hugo's most painful experiences. Realizing that he had become as invisible as the beggars at the traffic lights, shuffling between cars, their makeshift cardboard signs pleading for charity, he composed himself and walked out. He walked out, but he also swore, while pounding the bat on the pavement and staring up the length of the structure, that if he ever met the fucker, he'd get even with him, someway, somehow. And now, as he sat before Alexi, the day had finally come.

Dulce was off playing at the edge of the yard. Alexi was using a fork to serve himself a slice of Manchego cheese. And Hugo, while gripping the box cutter, took a deep breath and thrust out his pen. "And so we should begin," he said. "I'd like to know when you first knew this was a haunting. Every detail matters."

4

ALEXI PULLED OUT a bottle of Glenlivet XXV, poured two generous rations, and plopped into his seat. "To exterminating the fuck out of these evil spirits," he said, raising his glass. They toasted. Dulce spun around in circles, shouting, *"Wheeee!"* And Hugo sipped—only sipped. "$450 per bottle. You believe that? But I get a discount when I buy a case. What do you think? Good, huh?"

"I don't know," Hugo said. "It tastes like a week's salary." Then, certain that Alexi was watching, he poured the amber liquid out, still feeling the smoky sting of its crisp flavors.

"Hey! Hey!" Alexi shouted, jumping out of his seat, nearly toppling the table over at the sight of the scotch spilling. What did he plan to do? Catch it with his palms? Lap it up from the ground?

"For the orishas," Hugo said. He set his glass back on the table, made the sign of the cross.

Alexi made some unfortunate comments about the orishas and

voodoo dolls, making use of all the ill-informed stereotypes one would expect from such a man. Then he put down his glass, and only then did the attorney lean in to discuss the first encounter he'd had with a spirit.

So, Hugo listened intently—not like a man trying to understand something, but like one surveying a beach with a metal detector, unaware of the sunset and the pod of dolphins skirting the shore. In his eagerness to resolve the case, Hugo receded into his work. He imagined himself a machine, sorting through the ones and zeros of Alexi's bullshit, collecting only those tidbits that would suit him later and jotting them down. There was no need to become friends with the man—to see him as anything more than a face on a bus bench. All he needed were enough details to string together a convincing story. Only the right story, told well, would help resolve the situation.

ACCORDING TO ALEXI, the first supernatural encounter occurred on the day that the site's soil samples came back clean. Alexi drove to his property after court just in time to catch the excavator breaking ground on his future foundation. But in the dying embers of the day, the workers stopped short of completing the project, and this didn't sit well with him. In fact, when he confessed all of this to Hugo, he said, "You imagine what kind of attorney I'd be if I quit just 'cause the workday ended? I'll tell you why they half-assed that job." Alexi took one finger and stroked his forearm. Hugo was confused at first, until he realized that Alexi was referring to the color of their skin. Why Alexi felt comfortable making such a gesture in front of Hugo was anyone's guess. What was certain and clearly stated was that their skin color bothered him. He was racist. Of course he was. "Not even Afro-Cuban or Black or Indio. Haitian—the worst. I'm saving money with them, but am I?"

Listening to Alexi's story was difficult. Hugo could hardly breathe. But because he was a gifted listener, he was able to use his imagination to find comfort in all that Alexi hadn't said. Hugo pictured the workers stowing into their cars, preparing to join Miami's infinite stream of traffic. It was a comforting image, co-workers on their way home after an honest day's work. How Hugo wanted to be in one of those cars, driving away from Alexi and his forsaken plot of land—Hugo's own indebtedness nothing more than a passing lightning storm on the horizon, heading elsewhere.

"We should stay focused," Hugo said. "What about the spirit? Can you get to that part?"

Alexi said that he climbed out from his truck, stewing like some high-ranking member of la chucha comité. In his account, he noted that there was a flock of Florida parrots on his lot, squawking madly. These parrots usually quiet down when someone steps into their environment. They're brilliant animals, fully aware of the danger humans bring. But when Alexi stepped out of his truck, the parrots apparently didn't find him threatening. They continued squawking as he stumbled to the freshly dug pit. Hugo could almost picture it: Alexi waddling over his parcel of land.

"You inspected it?" Hugo asked. "The pit?"

"I did. I thought they'd started building my pool first."

"The pool? Why the pool?"

"I don't know."

"So, you're inspecting the pit," Hugo said. "What happens?"

"I got too close. I fell in."

A strange expression came over Alexi's face. It was as if he were reliving a waking nightmare. He hardly wanted to talk about it, but the scotch won over, and eventually he described the encounter in the greatest detail he'd offered yet. He passionately recounted what it felt like to be ankle-deep in mud, tripping over pieces of stone. It was raining, and there in front of him was another face: the devil itself. Ashen. Swollen. Cracked lips. Naked. Vulgar. Mouth wide open, a single tooth—a small tombstone, crooked in the gumline. Alexi struggled through the mud and away from the demon, but with every step, he sank further. The creature howled, or so he claimed. It trudged over to him, its eyes red as fired-up coals, and Alexi frantically tried to pull himself out. He was grabbing the soil, reaching for rock or root, anything that was anchored down. But the creature grabbed him by the ankle and dragged him back into the pit, searing him. And at this point, Alexi thought he might wake up—surely the demonic figure was of his imagination—but there was no waking from the nightmare. It thundered. A light rain proceeded. Alexi could feel his ankle raw and burned. He plodded desperately to the other edge of the pit, trying again to climb out. He could hear the creature smoldering behind him, each raindrop fizzing on its corpse. When Alexi finally escaped, out of breath, he instinctually gathered his legal composure and said, plainly, "I'm an attorney. You're on my property. Leave or I'll call the police." To his surprise, the tactic worked. The demon climbed out and left the site. Alexi only felt safe when the parrots, which had gone silent the moment the demon appeared, ventured out from the pine trees, squawking madly in the rain.

But it was another detail altogether that piqued Hugo's interest. When Alexi had described the demon departing, he'd noted that the creature had fallen into a violent phlegm-producing coughing attack. And hearing him describe this cough, Hugo remembered the mines—the condition that would infect the young, especially those who'd worked longest. It was a fleeting thought, and one that Hugo had no time to entertain further. He needed to reflect on Alexi's story, not his own.

"Where did the apparition go, then?" Hugo asked.

Alexi shrugged. "I don't know! I tried to find it again."

Emboldened, Alexi gazed out toward the now dark forest line. He walked closer. Nothing. No one. Suddenly, he wasn't sure whether he'd imagined it all, except that he was covered in mud, and when he pulled up his trousers and examined his ankle (likely under his flashlight app), he could see the singe from that creature's fiery fingers. "Even then, I didn't want to believe what was happening," Alexi confessed. "In fact, I didn't believe it." He went so far as to wonder whether some noxious gas had caused a hallucination. "But you had the soil tested," Hugo said. And Alexi nodded. "But you know *those* kinds of workers," he said, referring again to their skin color.

"So, the creature walked off. What'd you do next?" Hugo asked.

Alexi explained that he returned to his vehicle, flipped on the high beams, looked off into the tree line. Nothing. He waited, thinking the intruder might see the headlights and return, but as it got later, he gave up on his search and drove to his smaller (million-dollar) home, where his family was already asleep. He tiptoed up the stairs, undressed, climbed into his silk sheets, and scrolled through his phone. "This," he said, "was the first time I googled your botanica. I knew of it because my bookkeeper, Gloria, is into that kind of shit. In fact, she'd recommended I bless the land before building upon it. Maybe I should have." And having said this, Alexi rubbed his eyes and looked to the place on his property where the creature had surrendered, as if it might suddenly manifest.

A year would pass before Alexi would actually call Lourdes. In the meantime, he dismissed the incident. Or he tried to. But it haunted him to the degree that he stopped going to check in on his builders. Claudia would send him image boards on Pinterest—various pieces of furniture, color arrangements, textiles—but the thought of that creature roaming his home at night, dragging its limbs across the floor while they slept, made him consider backing out of the construction project altogether. Worse was that over time he began to realize he recognized the creature's face.

"Whose face was it?" Hugo asked.

Alexi refused to answer. "I still see her some nights. She's trying to warn me," he said.

"Warn you? About what?"

"I don't know. I've got no one to talk to. Claudia thinks I'm nuts. But I see her. I even smell her burnt skin. Don't you smell it now? Nowadays, I always smell it," he said, taking a whiff of the air. "Who am I kidding? You're the expert. You probably knew this already." Hugo nodded along slowly as if he truly possessed such powers, and at the very moment, before Hugo could answer,

Dulce leapt onto Alexi's lap. "Can I have some cheese?" He offered her his seat and a small plate.

～

AT HUGO'S REQUEST, he and Alexi set out to inspect the property. "I don't think I'm being haunted by just one ghost," Alexi said, undoing a shirt button and combing his arm hairs back with his fingernails. "I think it's a whole congregation of them. If such a thing exists."

What a strange word, Hugo thought, "congregation," as if these so-called spirits would actually gather to pursue a common cause. Hugo felt sorry for him—a grown man who still believed in ghosts. As Alexi described the "congregation," Hugo listened intently, picking up rocks, smelling them, and gradually leading Alexi further and further from the comforts of the pool deck.

What was Hugo doing? It was art and some improvisation. He hoped to elicit confusion. This was something Lourdes had inadvertently taught him. "The divine is never as interesting as the spectacle," she'd said, and though Hugo didn't entirely follow her reasoning, he understood the sentiment. He needed to remind his clients that the world is a mystical place, even if he didn't believe it. So he devised techniques such as this to disrupt the normal occurrences of daily life. And his gimmick worked. Alexi, who didn't take favorably to walking on the grass in his leather sandals, reluctantly followed along, clearly perturbed by the impromptu expedition through the lawn.

It took a while for Alexi to acknowledge Hugo's eccentric behavior. To his credit, he observed Hugo's strange rock-collecting practices respectfully, but when Hugo handed him a fistful to hold, he said, "Look now. I don't mean to be difficult here. But what are you doing, exactly?"

"Please! Hold these," Hugo said.

"I'd rather not . . . Whoa. Okay then."

"Piedritas."

"Sure. Whatever you want to call them."

"Let me explain to you," Hugo said, "how I'm going to evict your supernatural inhabitants. Because there are many. More than I'm used to seeing. You're right, Alexi. It's a congregation." Hugo had to look up at the clouds and stare for a moment, in order to fight off the smile and laughter rising within. "Most of my clients want to know how long this will all take, and frankly, as long as is necessary. But—and I say this knowing there are exceptions—usually three visits suffice."

"So, two more," Alexi said, handling the rocks in his hands.

"Not quite. Think of today as an initial consultation. I need to know what I'm dealing with."

"Do you know yet?"

"Not yet," Hugo said, scanning the property. "I'm going to need to learn more about your past—your history—to see if there are any skeletons in your closets, so to speak."

"I've got nothing to hide," Alexi said proudly.

"Good. Because I'll also need to conduct a thorough investigation of you now—the house, your family. Everything."

"You are most welcome."

"Finally, I'll need to learn more about your future."

"Future? Now there I can't help you. How would you even go about that?"

"I don't need to know the future. I just need to know your aspirations."

"Oh," Alexi said. "I'll save you the trouble. To make mountains of money."

They walked to the property's edge—a string of chain-link fence separating a sidewalk from the lawn. Hugo ran his fingers along the top of the fence and hummed a song to himself. Then he abruptly turned to Alexi. "One more thing. You have to trust me. All the way."

Alexi almost laughed. "I don't trust anyone," he said, handing back the rocks. "No offense."

"If you want this problem gone, you need to. I may ask you to do something you don't understand, and you may not have time to question it. You'll need to act as I say."

"I am willing to give anything a try, within reason," he said.

"Even without reason," Hugo shot back. "The spirits don't care about your reason."

"I understand. Okay. Whatever you say. Just make sure it works."

This was what Hugo had hoped to hear. Still, in his line of work, he'd learned that it was one thing for someone to say they'd "give anything a try," and another thing altogether for that person to actually follow through. Over time, Hugo had developed some strategies to test his clients' commitment. Fixing a haunting, or making someone believe that their home is cleansed, requires a sacred act—a sacrifice to Elegua, Lourdes might say. Usually, this involves the spilling of blood: severing a rooster's head, pressing a knife to a person's palm, or, for those who cannot stomach the blood, a pinprick. Only through sacrifice will Elegua allow passage into the divine. The sacrificial act is important in other ways, too. It's a symbolic gesture that tears a hole open in the way people live their lives. It's a bridge between the everyday and the supernatural. Hugo believes that the sacrifice alone is what leads to healing. For someone to feel saved, they must give something up.

"Have you planted any shrubbery on your property?" Hugo asked, scanning the lot.

"Shrubbery? Like bushes?" Alexi said. "We had the lot cleared when we built the house. Every plant and tree here is by choice."

"Show me. Take me to any of your landscaping features."

Alexi led Hugo to the front of the house, to some ferns cascading along the driveway, surrounding a magnificent bronze-looking fountain, with three spitting lions as its centerpiece. It was a lovely arrangement for someone as tacky as him and, clearly, the jewel of Alexi's landscaping profile. In such proximity to the fountain, Hugo could smell the faintly chlorinated water that always reminded him of indoor water parks. Without permission, Hugo trod into the ferns, careful not to trip over any of the electrical cords. He knelt in the greenery, digging through the soil with his bare hands. He went so far as to tear out fronds and fiddleheads, tossing them onto the driveway. He felt bad doing it, ruining a perfectly fine bit of landscaping, and he could sense Alexi's frustration. Sure, at first, Alexi watched passively, like all was well and normal in the world, but after a short while, when his growing befuddlement and annoyance could no longer be restrained, he yelled, "What the hell! Are you messing with me?"

Hugo paused, looked up, as if to say, *Out with it. What is it?*

"What are you doing to my plants?"

Hugo sat in the ferns. "I sensed something when I first arrived. Have you sensed it here?"

Alexi glanced at his watch. "No. Nothing in the ferns!"

"Close your eyes," Hugo said. "If you can relax, you may be able to feel it."

So, Alexi closed his eyes. He stood there, waiting for something. A minute later, he said, "I don't know what I'm supposed to be looking for. Can you give me a bit more direction here?"

"Step closer to me," Hugo told him. "But keep your eyes closed. Yes! Closer. Get your feet dirty. It's no big deal. Okay. Now slowly open your eyes. Do you see what I mean?"

"Not really," Alexi said. "Just seems to me like we're ruining my plants."

"Try this. Help me with this one thing. Put your hands in the soil and feel around for something that doesn't belong. It'll likely be a small wooden box, or a dozen or so cowrie shells."

"You want me to dig with my hands?"

"Yes. Feel through to the roots."

"Why would there be anything here?"

"Doubting already? I asked you to trust me."

Reluctantly, Alexi complied. He bent down at the waist, groaning—such bad form. Clearly, he'd never worked a day's hard labor in his life. Back in the mines, even children learned to bend at the knees. Never the back. As Alexi struggled to search through the shrubbery and the dirt, as he struggled to draw in his breath, Hugo moved on to his next phase. He reached into his satchel and delicately planted a small burlap bag into the soil. Lourdes had given it to him, prefilled with feathers and thirteen dog teeth.

Once he was certain it was deep at the plant's base, he yelled, "Jesus Christ! Come look!" Alexi hobbled over and knelt by his side. With a small stick, Hugo shoved the burlap pouch out from the dirt. "A curse," he yelled. "Somebody is definitely doing you harm."

Alexi reached for it, but Hugo swatted his hand away. "Are you stupid! Don't touch it."

"What do I know?"

"We have to break the curse before you can touch it."

"How do we break the curse?" he asked.

"You'll have to urinate on it, of course."

"Urinate?"

"Pee."

"Get the fuck out of here," Alexi said. "I'm an attorney. Absolutely not. It'll dry out the plant." But then something changed. As the good client he was learning to become, he shrugged, pulled down his zipper, said, "Fine. If it works," and he unraveled his shriveled little attorney dick from deep in his shorts and let out a steady stream right then and there, pungent and binding.

Watching him do this felt like some minor reparation for Hugo. Minor, yes, but he could feel retribution taking form. Better yet, as if the universe was in harmony with Hugo's ploy, one of Alexi's neighbors came by on an afternoon stroll; she was walking her dog, and two of her young boys were rollerblading beside her. Alexi was already midstream, and Hugo could tell he wanted to stop. His neighbor waved, friendly-seeming. She said, "Hi, Alexi! How is Claudia? You know . . ." And then she stopped speaking. The situation fully dawned on her before she could shield her children. They were already laughing. Alexi finished up and yelled, "Sorry! I'm really sorry." But the woman had already turned her back and was pulling her boys away.

Alexi zipped up and shoved Hugo. "I looked like an idiot!"

"The spirits," Hugo said, "don't care about your vanity."

"But I do," he said.

"You don't want to anger them more, do you?"

Alexi nodded; he was trying to be a good sport, and Hugo, to defuse the tension, congratulated him on a good pee, as if he were a child. "But do me a favor," Hugo said. "Don't shove me again. I understand that you're frustrated, but I ask for basic respect from you."

"Yes. You're right. I'm sorry."

"Thank you," Hugo said. "Now, please carry the pouch this way. Follow me."

Hugo popped his trunk, pulled out a large metallic bowl, blackened by fire. He tossed it on the driveway; it made a large clanging sound and whirled until it settled. "Pour the contents into the bowl. Do it carefully, ensuring that the items don't land on the ground. They must land in the bowl."

Alexi complied. The dog teeth rattled about, and when they settled, Hugo poured lighter fluid over them and set the contents ablaze. He'd imbued the teeth with copper sulfate, so they burned green, and this clearly impressed Alexi, who asked, "Do you see what's happening?"

Hugo chanted a song for Yemaya. It was in Yorùbá. Lourdes had taught him the song, and he didn't know what it meant, only that it was intended for the water goddess. While singing, he channeled Lourdes's passion. He uttered the words as if they were truly meant for Yemaya, and he did so, skeptic and all, because to perform the ritual in any other way would be disrespectful to Lourdes. He extracted a vial from his pouch, lifted it ceremonially, then poured its contents into the bowl until the flames were extinguished and the smoke engulfed the ashes. "The curse is broken."

"Is that it?"

"That's all. This isn't Hollywood. There aren't any special effects."

Alexi laughed. "So, was that little bag the cause of my haunting?"

"It is never so easy," Hugo said. "There's still a lot of dark energy in this house. Remember what I said. I will need to visit you three times to cleanse your home completely. And"—Hugo leaned into Alexi and whispered—"you said you'd clear my debt if I could do this, isn't that right?"

"Yes. Yes," Alexi said. "It's a simple thing."

Simple? Was it really? Something of that designation bothered Hugo in ways he didn't quite understand, and he was about to move on, but he found that he couldn't. Because he was thinking about Meli, how he'd always felt that maybe she resented how deeply in debt he'd become. He had to ask.

"Really? Simple?"

"Yeah."

"You know," Hugo said, "to be sure, I'll need that in writing."

"Sure. Of course. Let me just dig a little more . . . I just can't believe it," he said. "I was cursed. You think it was the Haitians? Those fucking Haitians." Alexi climbed further into his landscaping and proceeded to kick about the dirt. He dug around for a few minutes, tearing out his ferns by the roots, prepared to tear it all out, clearly convinced there were more hex bags buried in the patch.

Hugo wanted to laugh. It brought him such pleasure to watch the attorney on his hands and knees looking for magic in the dirt. In fact, though he didn't want to admit it, Hugo pitied him.

"Should I be using a stick?" Alexi asked, wiping his dirty hands on his linen shirt.

"It's okay," Hugo said. "You can stop. We found it. There are no more."

"I know I'm not supposed to touch the hex bags. Maybe I can use a shovel? Faster."

"Alexi, I really don't sense anything else here. I think you can stop now."

Alexi wasn't convinced. He dug more, and Hugo realized there was nothing he could say that would convince the man that there were no more curses. If it weren't for Claudia bounding up the driveway after her jog, stopping at the sight of her husband destroying the last of their nice-looking ferns, and asking, "Who's watching Dulce?" Alexi likely would have continued all evening.

5

CLAUDIA RAN TOWARD the unfenced pool with a speed and agility that Hugo hadn't thought she possessed. Had Dulce fallen in the pool? He'd thought it, and in doing so, he could picture it: that sweet child, facedown, a floating angel. The pain and terror, the funeral and burial, and the late nights of Alexi wandering the property, shovel in hand, trying to dig up more little curses. And Hugo! The regret he'd carry, having been so shortsighted that he'd let his revenge contribute to such parental neglect.

Hugo gripped his brother's old rosary. He always wore it on his wrist, looped around enough times to stay put. It was not a bulky item, and he seldom paid attention to it, but now he was pressing one of the beads as if for protection, even praying to the orishas. How he adored that little artifact from his past, the texture of its frayed leather and the scent of the stone and dirt. This string, now coming apart, was all that Hugo had kept when he left for the United States forever. It had protected him then, all those years ago, and now Hugo hoped that it would protect Dulce.

"She's not in the pool!" Claudia shouted. "Jesus Christ, Alexi! Where is she?"

Alexi responded to his wife's plea by tripping over something on the lawn and tumbling headfirst into the grass. When he fell, his linen button-up flapped over his face, flashing his barrel of a belly. Claudia entered their home. As Alexi fought to get on his feet, Hugo did not know what to do. He could hear Claudia shouting Dulce's name, and in that brief chaotic moment, he felt like he was part of their inner circle—not family, but something else. This moral obligation to protect Dulce, their child, surged within him, and to his surprise, Hugo proceeded to search, too, shouting, "Dulce! Everyone is worried. Where are you hiding?" Alexi joined him, and with dusk approaching, they might have seemed like dragonflies scouring the yard, chasing one mosquito after another.

They searched everywhere they could think to look: under the cars, in the hardest-to-reach corners of the garage, and even in each of the outdoor kitchen's cabinets. But Dulce was nowhere.

Rather than continuing the search, or taking a moment to regroup and consider a new course of action, Alexi grabbed Hugo's shirt, pulled him close, and said, "Did we cause this?"

"What?" Hugo asked, averting his eyes.

"When we broke the curse? Was this the cost?"

"We didn't do this," Hugo said.

"Did we anger the spirits? Have they taken my child?"

"Hey. Hey!" Hugo said. "Don't touch me."

Alexi shoved him against the wall, and he shouted, in tears, "He took her! He took her!"

That's when Claudia miraculously emerged from the house with Dulce. "She's safe."

Alexi abandoned his rage and Hugo's shirt, ran to his daughter, and embraced her aggressively, still crying.

"Okay. Okay already," Claudia said. "You're smothering her." She patted Dulce's head. "Can you please go pick up the toys you left out in the yard, my baby girl?"

They watched Dulce run off into the yard, oblivious to the terror she'd caused. Claudia collapsed onto a chair, poked at a slice of cheese—but seemed to think better of it—and said, "That was some mess you both made with the ferns. Really? This is what you did, babaláwo? Ferns?"

"Don't worry," Alexi said. "I'll have the landscape people come—"

"You think they'll be available . . . We're hosting Christmas, for fuck's sake."

"I'll make it worth their while."

"And Emily, down the street, texted me. Were you peeing in the yard? In the ferns?"

Alexi smiled. "Honey . . ."

"Peeing! In the yard," she said, and raised her hands toward heaven. "¡Jesucristo!"

"We were trying to—" Hugo said.

Claudia interrupted: "Well? Did you fix the problem? Have you sent the ghosts packing?"

"I'm confident I'll be able to help him with the spirits," Hugo said.

"Oh. Spirits. I thought it was a congregation," she said, laughing. "Which is it?"

"Do not offend him," Alexi said. "He is our guest, and he's a spiritual man."

"With all due respect," Hugo said, pointing his finger at Alexi, "you just attacked me."

"I don't believe it," Claudia said. "Alexi!"

"He pushed me," Hugo said. "I should leave."

Alexi looked to the stone floor, kicked around a dead carpenter bee. "It's these devils! They're driving me crazy. I'm sorry, Hugo. But did you know, Claudia, that just now we found—"

"Please," she said, interrupting him. "Please. Let's settle down. It's almost dinnertime. Would you care to join us, Hugo? We should feed you before you leave. Churrasco's on the menu."

This was not how Hugo wanted to spend his evening. He smoothed his tunic, looked at his phone. No text messages. No phone calls. Even if he spent the night alone, like he often did, he'd be happy to eat his white bean tuna salad in peace and cap the night off with some television. But then Alexi added, "If you stay, it'll give me some time to draw up our agreement. Full debt cancellation, right?" Alexi moved on to clearing the table: the platter, the tumblers. And Hugo, to help, picked up the utensils, the leftover charcuterie, and said, "Dinner sounds good! Thank you!"

⌒

AFTER HER SHOWER, Claudia threw a clean linen tablecloth over an outdoor table; she set the plates. Dulce helped with the utensils. Hugo sat at the outdoor bar, drinking a beer and watching Alexi marinate the skirt steaks. "Siri, play my Patio Beats Playlist 2," Alexi said. Then, hands deep in meat, he said, "I had Alexa for a while. Didn't work for someone with my name," he said, and he laughed, deep. "Claudia used to yell at me, 'What the hell, Alexi?' And Alexa would come to my defense with phrases like 'Sorry, I'm having trouble understanding you right now.' And this one time, I swear, Claudia accuses me of letting one loose, and you know what Alexa says? She says, 'If you're the denier, you must be the supplier.'" Alexi laughed real good with that story, and so did Hugo. Really, it wasn't so bad, being a guest in the Ramirez household, even if the day's events had been bizarre. And while Hugo sat, enjoying the pleasures of having others prepare food for him, he realized that he'd forgotten about his indebtedness entirely. Was this what it would be like to be debt-free? He finished his beer, helped himself to another. Then he and Alexi fired up the grill and cooked the steaks. Claudia put the finishing touches on a baby kale salad, fresh from a Florida City farm, and soon they were all seated at the table, some '90s jams playing softly in the back, the sound of traffic muffled and far off.

Dulce sat at the table with a Target catalogue, marking off toys she hoped Santa would bring her. Claudia was helping her when Alexi interrupted to say grace. Dulce, knowing the ritual, put her catalogue away, facedown, and lifted her drink. Hugo followed her cue, and Alexi said, "Bless us and this bounty that we have received through Christ. Amen." Everyone repeated "Amen," and just as Hugo was lifting his fork and knife, Alexi said, "Well, it's not every day that we have such a spiritual man at our table."

He smiled, holding his drink. "Would you like to add something, Hugo?"

He did not. He'd never been someone to say grace, but feeling good and a little buzzed, and watching the neighbors' twinkling Christmas lights sway in the breeze off the palm trees, he said, "Sure," and he lifted his drink and said, "To a beautiful and kind family. And to you, too, Alexi."

Claudia gave out a good laugh.

Dulce tugged at her mom's blouse. "What's so funny?"

And Alexi clinked glasses with Hugo and said, "You've got a sense of humor, don't you?"

So, they ate, and the food was plentiful. The meat was wonderfully flavored. With each bite, Hugo could feel the iron and oil going directly into his bloodstream. When was the last time he'd eaten this way? He'd drunk so much and felt so comfortable on the patio that he helped himself to three generous servings. Dulce, who could not sit still through even the first course, eventually took her toy catalogue and lay out by the patio's edge to further round out her list. It seemed, for a moment, like Alexi might reprimand her, but Claudia put up her hand and said, "Let her be."

When dinner ended, Hugo volunteered to help clear the table, but Alexi and Claudia insisted that he relax and enjoy the rest of his drink. But instead of sitting at the table, he knelt and sat on the stone floor, by Dulce. Seldom was he around children. "Hi," he said. "Find anything cool?"

"Yeah," she said, bashfully. She made no eye contact and flipped through the book.

"Do you have a favorite toy?"

At this question, Dulce smiled widely, endearing herself to Hugo with her missing front teeth, and she turned to her favorite toy wildly, tearing a page of the catalogue in the process. She pointed to the Barbie Dreamhouse. "I really like this. I want one. I'm going to ask Santa for it," she said. "Even Rocio likes it. She says, 'But, Dulce, you *already* live in a big giant dream house.' She's so funny!"

"Wow! What a cool toy. You think Santa will bring it?"

"Yeah! He'll bring it. I'm good. I'm a good girl."

"What does Rocio want from Santa?" Hugo asked.

Dulce giggled. "Silly. Santa wouldn't bring her anything."

"Why not?"

"She's not a kid. She's an old woman."

"An older woman? Like your grandmother?"

"No!" Dulce shouted, exasperated now. "She's the old woman in the walls."

"Oh." Hugo smiled, though Dulce's comment startled him. "So she's your friend?"

"Yeah, she is. She's so nice. She says I already live in a dream house. Don't I?"

"You sure do," he said. He stood and stretched his legs with a walk around the pool. *What a wild imagination*, he thought. Like father, like child. It all reminded him of his own youth—of those days back in Omaha when he would spend hot and lonely summer afternoons playing with his brother in the yard, or pretending to. It would make Santiago, the man who raised him, so mad, but Hugo loved using his imagination. What better way to keep his brother's memory alive.

AT THE END of the evening, with Claudia and Dulce upstairs and in bed, Alexi led Hugo to his private study. "Yes. Yes," he said, pushing the door open. "We still have business to attend to. Please sit."

So, Hugo did, in a brown leather chair across from a luxe modern office desk. The study was quite small, for such a mansion, so Alexi had to scoot against the wall to get behind the desk. Perhaps the room had been intended, at some point, to serve as some kind of walk-in utility closet. There were no windows, and the decor! It was nothing like the rest of the house. There was something of a vomitty fraternity to it—the only kind, the cliché kind, that Hugo had seen on TV. It was clear that Alexi had claimed this room as his. Up on the wall, right behind his desk, hung one of his old bus-bench ads. Seeing it there—the old Alexi, pristine—made Hugo want to talk about Meli.

"Those ads," he said. "I remember when they were everywhere. It's been years."

"Yes, they were," Alexi said proudly. "They were my friend Gloria's brainchild. She said the whole thing came to her in a vision. And look. I don't believe in that stuff. But it worked out, no?"

"And now I know the story behind the bus bench," Hugo said.

"Okay. Look here." He swiveled his computer monitor and directed Hugo's attention to some sort of database. Hugo could see the names of many, many people, alongside their debt totals, and he was astounded at the sheer volume: tens of thousands of debtors, if not more. How many millions of dollars had been sold off by credit card companies or hospitals to companies like Alexi's?

As Alexi scrolled, searching for Hugo's debt profile, the rapport they'd developed slowly dissolved.

"There we go," Alexi said, clicking loudly. "Hugo Contreras, $68,173.15. Is that right?"

Hugo nodded.

"That's a lot of money," Alexi said. "Let me see here. Mostly medical."

"Look, I've been paying for a decade. You garnish my wages," Hugo said.

"Yes. I see that here. $515 per month. I'm curious. Why didn't you file for bankruptcy?"

"I almost did," Hugo said. "But it didn't feel right. It felt—"

"Really? I would have," he said, and smirked. "In your shoes, of course."

"It felt unfaithful."

"Let me see what I could do."

Alexi flipped the screen back toward himself and proceeded to tap away at the keys. Hugo didn't know what was going on, and he feared that Alexi—having seen how much he owed—would walk back his offer. Hugo didn't think his services were worth nearly $70,000 in debt forgiveness.

It all seemed too good to be true until Alexi's printer spit out a contract.

"Okay. I'll explain these terms," he said.

Hugo nodded, and he leaned in to read the document, following the tip of Alexi's pen for reference. It was an oblique document, jammed with clauses and conditions. Attorney bullshit. As Alexi proceeded to review the conditions, Hugo became nervous. He didn't understand a spit of what was coming out of Alexi's mouth. Sinking under the language, he interrupted and said, "Look, we don't have to read through the whole thing. I just need to know that if I take care of this haunting for you, I won't owe you a thing. The debt will be canceled, right?"

Alexi seemed to process what Hugo had said, then nodded. "Yes. It'll be canceled, but I need to know the haunting has ended. The burden of providing that proof rests with you."

"So, I have to fix the haunting. Then prove to you that I fixed it."

"Yes."

"Then I'm debt-free."

"Then you're debt-free."

"What stops you from claiming it's not over?"

"Hugo. Hugo," he said. "Trust goes both ways. Just fix it, okay?"

AFTER SIGNING THE document and securing the retainer, Hugo was escorted to his car. Once outside, he felt that he'd forgotten something. Looking through his notebook, he remembered. "Oh. You said something earlier. You said that you knew who the spirit that you encountered in the pit was."

"That's right."

"Can you please elaborate? This information could be very helpful."

"I don't know if it would mean much to you," he said. "But it was the face of a woman I'd won a judgment against. Actually, the first person that my law firm collected on. She was so good about making her payments on time. She used to send in little handwritten checks, even though she could have paid online or by phone, or she could have had her payment automatically deducted, but she insisted on paying by check. You believe that? I could always fish out her envelopes from the mail because they were pink, and they had little roses at the border. And she'd write her name nice and big at the top left-hand side of the envelope. It's tragic what happened to her. Her house burned down—in the middle of the night—and firefighters found her remains the next day."

"God. That's terrible."

"I know. She was such a nice lady. Her estate never did cover her debts."

"How do you know it was her?" Hugo asked.

"I think I'd recognize my first debtor."

"But you said that she was burned and ashen."

"Look. It was Rocio Gutierrez. I'm sure of it."

Rocio! Dulce's imaginary friend? Suddenly, Hugo didn't feel like being at Alexi's anymore. He thought he could feel the specter. No. No. Dulce must have heard her father say that name, he rationalized. There was nothing to fear. Demons, spirits, werewolves— they could all be explained.

"When can I expect to hear from you?" Alexi asked.

"Tomorrow," Hugo said. "I'll need to do a walk-around of your house."

"Don't bother with an appointment. Just come over. Any time after dinner. Eight p.m.?"

"Great. Tomorrow then. We'll get this all sorted out before you know it."

"I hope we do," Alexi said and shook his hand. And as Hugo reversed off the property, he couldn't help but feel that something was missing. What was it? He had the retainer, the contract, and he felt nourished and in good spirits. It wasn't until later, driving home, that he realized none of Alexi's outdoor lights had been turned on. While he was on the dark highway, something altogether strange began to stir in him. It was a feeling that someone was in the car with him. Rocio? Maybe he was spooked. Listening to his clients' paranoid ramblings tended to put Hugo on edge. Of course there was nobody with him. Even when he tilted the rearview mirror back just to check, he was not surprised to see that he was utterly alone. But the feeling persisted, and eventually he pulled over on the side of the highway, under some massive overpass, and he gave the car a good inspection, just to be sure. The thing is, Hugo wanted there to have been someone. He wanted Meli. He wished for a child. He hated that he was alone in the world, and standing there as cars sliced past, he almost cried. It felt nonsensical. He was mourning the family he'd never had. He resented Alexi for parading his beautiful wife and daughter before his eyes, a family squandered on a man like that.

Hugo imagined what his own daughter would be like, how on school days she'd run out to wait for the bus with all the neighbors' kids, cute in her little school uniform, and how she'd wrap her arms around his neck to wish him goodbye. He could picture taking her to Lourdes's botanica. Lourdes would often give children suckers, and Hugo could imagine his daughter touring the store with her own little lollipop. He dreamed of Christmas mornings, his little girl running into the living room, thrilled because Santa had come—she'd been good. How he wished to re-create the magic Santiago had given him those cold mornings. And as he brought this nonexistent child to life in his imagination, he felt so sad at the world she would never know, and the life he would never have. So, he got back in his car, and he drove away, half imagining that if he looked in the rearview mirror, he'd see her under the overpass. And when he did look back, he had to rub his eyes and shake his head because he swore he did see her, though when he looked again, there was no one there.

6

LIKE MOST PEOPLE in their generation, Meli and Hugo fucked around *a lot* before they met, which was why, when they first got serious with each other, they visited Planned Parenthood and got tested for every sexually transmitted disease on the books. They were astounded when the nurse came back to them with two squeaky-clean bills of health. It was a miracle, they believed, to come out of their promiscuity unscathed. To celebrate, they went to the McDonald's on 125th Street. Meli ordered a McRib; Hugo ordered a nine-piece Chicken McNuggets meal and a vanilla Oreo McFlurry to share.

When they were seated and midway through their meal, Meli blurted out, "Not even herpes! We're so lucky." The café, on that particular day, was unusually quiet. She'd spoken so loudly that the cashier/manager had overheard her remarks, and he was appalled. A few booths over, a young woman trying to get her two children to eat their food shot Hugo a look as if to say: *I'm with my kids. Do you mind not fucking talking about herpes?* "Babe," Hugo said, "not so loud, okay?"

"Please," she said, sucking her teeth. "Nobody here speaks English."

"Why do you got to say stuff like that? You sound like your aunt."

"Listen! What if I'd had something?" she asked. She bit into her McRib, nodded her head. "Would you . . . ?" she said, and she took another bite, breaking eye contact with Hugo.

"Would . . . ?"

"Would you still be with me if I had an STD?"

"Yes, of course," Hugo said.

"Well, I'd dump your ass," Meli said, and she kicked him under the table and laughed, and then, because that wasn't enough, she threw a couple of French fries at him and said, "Loser." Then she threw some more, nearly knocking the McFlurry over. Hugo didn't appreciate her joke at all.

"You ever catch anything now," she added, "I'll know it's 'cause you're cheating."

"Meli! I would never."

The cashier/manager came by and said, "If you can't be respectful in here, I'll need you to leave. This is a family establishment." When he walked away, Meli erupted with laughter. The way she lit up—head up high, confident-seeming—terrified Hugo. Was she not in the least concerned that they'd be kicked out? Still, he loved the way that Meli could always, unabashedly, be herself.

As the cashier/manager attended to new customers, Meli took her red Sharpie and tagged "Meli & Hugo 4 life" on the plastic seating, careful not to draw much attention. She made the *o* in "Hugo" a heart. "Now you," she said, handing over the Sharpie. "Or do you not love me for life?"

"Meli! You're crazy," Hugo said. He was not the rebellious kind. He already stood out, and he hated to do anything that called even more attention to himself. Maybe it was because he'd spent six years feeling like the only brown person in Omaha. Even when he got to Miami, Hugo was not recognized as Bolivian but as Indio. Anyone from South and Central America was. He felt it sharply around Meli's family, the way her aunt could so casually say things like, "Niña, tienes que mejorar la raza," as if he were not there on her couch, "el Indio," as Lena liked to call him.

He sipped from his soda, nervously, and then seized the marker and drew a little heart over the *i* in "Meli," though in his haste it looked more like a blob. "I love you, Meli," he said. "You're about to get us kicked out of McDonald's, but I'd rather be here with you than anywhere else."

"Aww, Hugo! You always say such nice things. Don't you have a mean bone in your body?"

Meli was right. Hugo had a knack for saying nice things. Months before their wedding, they were going on evening strolls through their neighborhood, dreaming of home ownership and trying to sweat away the pounds. Meli wanted to slim her waist; Hugo wanted to fit into his slacks. They'd been fantasizing about wealth and success and going back to school, and somehow Meli got to complaining about her birth control. Maybe it was because it had rained—and so the neighborhood was infested with swarming gnats—but Meli was in a bad mood. At work, she'd read a clickbait article about a woman whose birth control medication had made her allergic to red meat; it also resulted in an unwanted pregnancy.

Meli worked part-time at the Banana Republic outlet, and to make matters worse, Priscilla, one of her coworkers, had told Meli that birth control causes blood clots and brain aneurysms—worse than vaccines. Hugo could see that Meli was overwhelmed. She was convinced her birth control was killing her. She was convinced she was going to get pregnant, even if they were being careful. She didn't want to be a mom. She didn't want to be an aunt. Judging by her demeanor, by her accelerated pace and the way she was swinging her arms wildly—not even looking both ways before crossing streets—Hugo could see that Meli was distraught. Before she could go on for long about birth control, Hugo stopped her. They were in some stranger's driveway—the guy in his truck clearly waiting for them to pass so he could leave. Hugo took Meli's hands in his and said, "I'll get a vasectomy for you." He even dropped to one knee as if he were proposing all over again. This, he thought, was rebellious, but it made her family resent him even more, for being less of un hombre.

It was an expensive procedure, but Hugo went through with it anyway. Afterward, he complained that it felt like a kick in the balls. "But don't you feel sexier now," Meli said, "like in a super progressive way? I mean, I think you're sexier now. How many dudes would do that?"

"I don't know if 'sexy' is the right word," Hugo said, ice pack between his legs.

"But look. Mira. Now we can fuck whenever without fear of disease or little monstrous children. I don't know about you, but I'd say this is a major freaking win in our relationship."

"It is."

"But don't you go sleeping around now. Don't fuck it up."

"Meli!" Hugo said. "I can't believe you'd even think that."

"Well, good. How about we *do it* right now," she said, rubbing the length of him, arousing him so that it hurt. Maybe Hugo regretted the vasectomy, but even if he wanted kids, they couldn't afford them, so, privately, he came to accept his station in life, the efficiency they'd likely always live in, the crappy car they'd probably own until its engine fell off, and the dead-end jobs they'd always hold on to. It wasn't a luxurious life, but it wasn't exactly bad. They were happy for a while. Then Hugo did betray her. Something awoke in him that he could not control. She never found out, but he could follow their problems to that original transgression, the only real haunting he'd ever known. And now, though Hugo did not believe in the spiritual, he was beginning to wonder whether Meli, in death, knew what he'd done. Once, in a dream, she walked into the efficiency's bedroom, gasping for breath. She was in the emerald dress she'd been laid to rest in, covered in dirt. When she caught her breath, she sat on the bedside and said, "For life, huh? You're so full of shit, Hugo."

PART II

THE
RAMIREZ
CHRISTMAS
EVE PARTY

7

HUGO FUMBLED WITH his key and his flashlight app, and when he was ready to push into his little home, something horribly familiar caught his attention. Perhaps the breeze had brought him the fragrance of some nearby jasmine blooms. Yes, he thought. A chance breeze. So he touched the doorknob and, feeling her cold humid skin on his fingertips, retracted his hand forcefully, as though he'd just been burned by a still-hot pan. He remembered her as she was *that* day, stiff, mouth agape, eyes wide open, a single housefly probing her tears. It was such a shocking vision. He felt, in that instance, like Meli was actually there—a walking corpse, back from the grave, breathing on his neck. He could *feel* her presence. Notes of jasmine and patchouli blossomed on his front porch, but there was more. Something in the vicinity was decaying—a sweet iron-rich scent, a warm softness.

The day she died, the white sheets were so crimson that the blood seemed like red palm oil. Hugo kept dabbing his fingers in it, hardly able to believe his eyes. Soon the sugar ants found her, and they swarmed. He could not stop them from feeding. It took him weeks to fully acknowledge what had occurred in his bedroom, and when he did, he cried and cried until he blocked out the incident. So, when he thought of Meli, he'd begin as far away from the incident as he could: the day they met. A chance encounter at a nightclub. A walk along the beach, followed by dinner at a late-night cafeteria. Meli was amazed that he'd been at a nightclub by himself, and he felt special, that she would leave her friends to be with him. Those were the days, early in their courtship, that he wanted to hold on to. Not how it all ended. With time, Hugo obliterated the unpalatable memories and replaced them only with happy ones, until Meli was some idyllic version of who she'd really been.

But on this night, upon touching the doorknob, which felt to him cold like the flesh of her corpse—and upon remembering Meli's ossified expression, how he'd tried and failed, many times, to close her mouth before the paramedics arrived—he felt a surge of remorse course through his body, and he swore, standing there, that he could actually feel Meli's hands caressing his back, as she had done countless times in the warmth of their small bedroom, the television screen lighting the room.

Hugo did not want to turn around. What if he did and she wasn't there? Would he ever find the strength to stop looking for her? And what if, worse, he turned, and she was actually there?

A car passed slowly. Shadows splashed on the wall. It was enough of a distraction to calm his nerves. After that, he chuckled, and even though he was nervous, he turned to face her, or whatever it was that had caused such a rise in him. There was nobody there, of course. Hugo knew better than to believe in ghosts. Meli was dead. He pushed into his home and locked the door.

~

ALL WAS AS he'd left it: the single coffee mug on the drying rack, the half-empty glass of water on the kitchen table, the un-opened mail in the trash bin. All except for the chair—Meli's chair. The one at the breakfast nook, which he hadn't sat on since she'd passed away. It was pushed against the wall.

Had he done that—scuffed the wall? He didn't know. Perhaps in the rush to get to work on time, he'd bumped into the chair by accident, though this seemed unlikely. He wasn't the kind of person to be so negligent. It looked like the kind of thing that Meli would do. In fact, seeing the chair butting up against the wall made something rise up deep in Hugo. He felt an invigorating urge to complain, to yell, "Coño, Meli! Be more aware. Why you got to mess up the wall all the time?"

He could almost hear her response: "You're acting like we own the place." Hugo pushed the chair in.

Something else caught his attention. On his tabletop, there was a Pottery Barn catalogue addressed to her. Yes. Even though she'd passed away, the corporations kept those catalogues coming. Usually, he tossed them in the trash right away. He was not the kind of person to care about furnishings. It mattered little to Hugo whether a table was made of walnut or medium-density fi-berboard. He had no preference between cotton or polyester, which was why it caught him by surprise when he found himself not only holding the catalogue open but flipping through it, too, moving from a modern cabinet to a more rustic one with dark wood and iron. This, he thought, admiring the ornate armoire, would look great in the living room. He could almost picture Meli nodding in approval.

How strange, to suddenly have an urge to spruce up the place, maybe buy some new linens, a matching set of plates and utensils, some artwork. But why? It wasn't as if he ever hosted parties. He hosted no one. These things were all in Meli's purview, yet feeling Alexi's contract in his pants pocket, he thought, *You know what? Maybe I will do something about the place. If I can get through this job, maybe I'll have enough cash to splurge, and why shouldn't I?* He wanted to spend money. The thought infected him. He couldn't bear it, the need for a transaction. He knew he was still plugged into Alexi's machine. Next paycheck, his wages would be garnished, and frustrated by this realization, he tossed the catalogue in the trash. *What am I thinking? Who cares?* And even though he was by himself, he could picture Meli storming off to the bedroom, disappointed by his frugalness.

It was in this befuddled state that Hugo changed into his old pajamas and retired for the night. He didn't even turn the television on. He was too tired. He lay in bed, in a room that could have been mistaken for a tomb. He waited for his indebtedness to climb into bed with him, and he turned to it as if to spoon. "I'm sorry," he whispered. "I'm so fucking sorry." In the dark, he felt the weight of its leg. He felt its hand touch his face, or maybe that was merely his exhaustion, slowing his heart rate down, deepening his breathing, until he had mellowed out and was fully asleep.

THE NIGHT WOULD have ended there, but Hugo was awoken at 12:07 a.m. by a stomachache. It must have been the food, he thought—too rich. He tried drinking water, but that only made him feel worse. Eventually, he buckled over the toilet and forced himself to puke up his dinner. As he did so, he could hear thunder off in the distance, just another Florida storm, and there was something else, a disquietingly familiar voice coming through the wall like a whisper. "¿Estás bien, hombre?"

Hugo responded by saying that he was fine. Just something he ate that didn't sit well. He thanked the voice for its concern and insisted that whoever it was not worry. He'd be okay. He also apologized for waking them up, and he reiterated that it likely sounded much worse than it was.

"No seas un depre."

"¿Depre? ¿Quién habla?" Hugo shouted.

There was no answer.

"¿Puedes oírme? Who is speaking?"

In his state, somewhere between exhaustion and being jostled awake, Hugo believed he was imagining things. *That voice*, he thought. *I know that voice.* And then it hit him. Those words. They were something Santiago had once said. But that was a long time ago, somewhere between Córdoba and Apizaco. They'd eaten canned pinto beans for dinner, and Hugo had vomited all of it on the train tracks. It was an unfortunate situation. They were running low on food and cash. The trek to the United States was proving to be a perilous one. Santiago, likely frustrated or overwhelmed by the journey, had taken a stick and poked at all the vomited-up bits of food, as if some of it were salvageable. And while he was doing this, he'd said, "Joder, hombre. No seas un depre." He cleaned Hugo's mouth with a rag, offered him some water, and commanded, "Hay que seguir." Back then, Hugo hadn't decided whether he could trust him. He was a stranger—a white man simply paying off a debt to Hugo's *real* father—and who could say Santiago wouldn't abandon him altogether?

But when he remembered Santiago, or Santi, as he came to call him, indifferent and poking at the puke with a stick, and when he remembered the hardness of the earth, and the exhaustion—so many days walking along the tracks, hungry, burning under the sun, crying because he'd left everyone he'd ever loved—when the immensity of his past surged through him, he had to sit down at the edge of his bed. It was then, staring at a blank wall, that he wondered, for the first time in his adult life, *How have I traveled so far from home?* And there was something else stirring in the dark, with the light pitter-patter of rain on the rooftop—the rumbling thunder of his youth, at first silent but then really beginning—and as the storm raged, he lay in his bed, closed his eyes, and just like that, he felt something grab his hand and pull him off the bed and into the dark. "Is that you, Meli?" he asked. He was dreaming, he thought. How else could he be transported from his bedroom to a mountain road with nothing around except for a stone shelter stark against the blistering sun?

FROM THE MOUNTAIN path, Hugo could see the great expanse of a city, a mess of a place, a terra-cotta and gravel-

speckled modernist painting—so many lines and slopes and bustling streets crammed into a valley region. He gazed out upon
patched rooftops, rising smoke, bell towers, so unlike the fast-
food signs and billboards splayed across every inch of Miami-
Dade. The colonial city looked of a different era. Hugo wondered
if maybe he'd seen a panorama of it in some screen saver or some
bingeable television show. Had Marvel filmed one of their block-
busters here? Michael Bay? He could almost picture the Decepti-
cons raining steel and hellfire down upon it all. In this way, the
city was no more than some disposable apparition. Hugo felt no
affinity with it; he remembered nothing of his home.

Not right away, at least. It took him some time while wandering through the oxygen-thin air to feel the familiar pangs of his
childhood, the metallic flavor on his tongue, the light-headedness.
He saw the stone and boulders on the inclines, miraculously held
in place, and la yareta, thriving, so green and globular along the
path. He'd been here before. He was sure of it. When he reached
down and ran his fingers, cautiously, against the many cool blossoms of la yareta, his older brother's face rose into his mind. He
remembered running barefoot down the mountain, feeling the
heat on the stones. On hot days, he remembered a game he'd
play—when he and his brother would race boulders down the
inclines. Sometimes, when they were done, they'd press their feet
into la yareta's blossoms, and they'd lie back on the dry mountain
and watch the clouds stream by—"to the United States," his
brother loved to say. "Like us. One day we'll ride those clouds all
the way to Miami!"

Those endless and meandering days were from a time long
ago, so lost in Hugo's memories that he was surprised he could

excavate them at all. "Victor!" he shouted, half expecting to see his brother bound forth from the path, young, lanky, a mop of hair covering his eyes. He remembered the little strip of peach fuzz on his brother's upper lip, the wisp of a mustache, which seemed, then, profoundly mature. And he remembered the way that Victor would always wear his sweaters loose, the sleeves too long and flailing around clumsily. And though years had passed, he wanted to be Victor's little brother again, to traverse that mountain path with him once more. But his brother was not there. When Hugo called out for him, his voice was met only by the wind and the shadows of the clouds streaming along the desert mountainscape, and by the memory of Victor in a coffin.

Hugo followed the mountain road, and although more than thirty years had passed since he'd felt the chalk of stone on his lips, it was all coming back to him. He could have walked the roads blindfolded and found his home. There it was, a stone structure nestled between two weathered and barren desert oaks. Affixed to one of the oak's branches, a variety of three-gallon plastic containers, which Hugo and Victor would use to bring water up the mountain. Littering the floor were pieces of wood and cardboard that they'd collected throughout their childhood and would play with. Stacked neatly by the door were their madrina's baskets, all spindly and frayed, which she'd make from twigs and wild grass. It was a poverty-stricken home, a hand-me-down from one of the many mining companies their madrina had been affiliated with. Widows were often looked after by the mining companies. Their madrina, who could barely climb the slope without getting winded, was a "security guard" on the books—a woman tasked with preventing thieves from entering the mines.

The company had given her a rifle, which she kept under her bed alongside a box of bullets.

For Hugo, she was the closest thing to a mother. She was "madrina" in public, but at home she was "Mima," and she loved her boys very much. And seeing her at home, the smoke rising from the stovepipe, Hugo hastened his stride, faster, until he was running. Why had he ever left her?

When Hugo, finally, pushed through the door, he saw Mima there, standing over the woodstove, stirring a pot of stew. There were feathers in a tin bucket. She was cooking quail!

"Mima!" he shouted. "Mima! Is it really you?" She was dressed in a long red skirt, a tan-colored shawl around her shoulders, her dark hair heavy and down to her waist. Beside her there was a cutting board, a few bunches of herbs. Hugo eased up next to her, said, "Hola, madrina. Don't you recognize me? It's me. Hugo." She didn't acknowledge him. *I must be dreaming.* He took comfort in this thought, and he sat on a pile of wood near the stove and took it all in: the smell of the quail stew, the last of the daylight, the woven garlic hanging above the stove. When the soup was done, Mima set the table, and—because the sun was setting—she lit a candle and sat, patiently waiting.

Surely she was waiting for the boys to get home. But as the night carried on, it became painfully clear to Hugo that nobody was coming. Mima said grace, as she always had, and then she ate, and when she was done—when she'd slurped down the last bit of soup—she pushed her bowl of bones away, tossed her spoon, and stared out the window, while the mountain air filled the home.

Hugo felt as though it were his fault. He should have been there. He knelt by her side, caressed her cheek. "Mima," he whispered, "please don't cry. I'm here. I've always been here." But he knew that was a lie, too. He hadn't been there. He'd gone to the US at nine, started a new life, and he'd forgotten. He'd buried his life on the mountain under indifference and petty experiences at school or with Santi or at the botanica. He'd lived his life as if there had never been any origin to it.

Mima was distraught. She covered her face with her hands and howled while the candle flame she'd lit danced wildly—like a witch's candle, fighting back all of the demons of the night.

It pained Hugo that he could do nothing to ease her grief. He wanted to leave. He wanted to wake from his nightmare. "Get me out of here!" he yelled, but who would listen? Who had taken him there to begin with? And as he tried, fruitlessly, to will himself awake, he noticed that something was beginning to seem off. In the corner where he and Victor had always slept, everything was missing—their toys, clothing, school supplies. "Mima, what did you do with our things?" he asked.

In a way, he was speaking to himself. He'd come to terms with the logic of his dream, so it startled him when, upon turning to face his madrina, he saw her staring right at him. She was holding a Coca-Cola bottle filled with wildflowers, which Hugo had left her on the day he departed.

"Jesus Christ," Hugo said. "You scared me. So you can see me?" And when he said this, he heard voices outside, and he felt a searing fire, and he saw seven devils—all ashen and burning— slink into the home from every opening. They were beasts, standing on four legs with long heavy tails that whipped around. Some crawled right through the door. One entered by the window. Another burrowed beneath the stove. One sidled up beside him, held his hand—a touch he registered instantly: his indebtedness. And in an instant, they descended on her, ruthlessly, and fed on her. They bit and crunched on her bones and tore her skin until there was nothing left behind except the Coca-Cola bottle rolling on the ground. And when they were done, after they panted and licked their claws, they turned to Hugo, and they opened their mouths and screeched with such an intensity that Hugo fell back and through the wall and into his own bed, thousands of miles and decades away. By then, the storm had subsided. Hugo shot up in bed and turned on the lights.

It was just past three a.m.; the A/C was purring.

And now Hugo could not go back to sleep. To ease his mind, he reached for Alexi's contract, unfolded it, and proceeded to read the fine print. Words like "caveat emptor" and "force majeure" and all the regular attorney bullshit made the document so obtuse, as if Alexi had designed it to conceal as many loopholes and vagaries as possible. It was a dry document, but it didn't distract him as he'd hoped. He wasn't even really reading it. Sure, he was following the letters, pausing at every period, even rereading lines, but he couldn't get the metallic taste out of his mouth. He could still feel the chalk on his lips, smell his madrina's soup. He wished he'd written to her or sent postcards or called on the day he graduated from high school. The thought had crossed his mind before, and certainly there were nights when he'd remember her brusque voice, the way she'd tuck him and his brother in at night, telling stories of the devil in the mountain. He wondered if his madrina was still alive. And he worried about what he'd find if he actually went looking.

WHEN HUGO AND MELI first moved into the efficiency, it was supposed to be a temporary thing. They were going to get their life together, then maybe even buy their own little place somewhere in the far reaches of West Kendall. It was August, and because the efficiency didn't yet have air-conditioning—not even a box unit—they decided in the evening to sit in the narrow grassy corridor between their home and the neighbors' slotted fence. Slick in bug spray and trying to take advantage of whatever cool breeze the night could bestow on them, Meli leaned in and said, "I want to know something. Why don't you ever talk about your mom? I don't even know her name."

Cocuyos flicked their green lights about them. They were beautiful from afar, though they looked like little roaches up close. Hugo did not understand why people in Miami were so enamored with them. They'd snap their bodies if they got scared, which made a horrible cracking sound. Meli hated them especially. With one crawling up her leg, Hugo said, "I don't remember her."

"There's got to be something," she said. "Maybe a sound? A sensation?"

"I don't like talking about this stuff. I really don't."

Meli sipped from her juice. She settled back in her chair, and she didn't push the issue any further. She respected him. But that night, they found nothing else to discuss, so they watched the cocuyos fumbling about in the neighbors' tangled bougainvillea tree until Hugo said, "You know, there is something. My brother used to talk about her. I think he was maybe three when she left us."

She stroked his arm, "Why did she leave?"

"She just did."

"And your father?"

"Look, Meli, here's what I know about my mother. She was mestiza and darker than us."

"Mestiza?"

"Yeah. You know. Like mixed race."

"Sure. I knew that."

"Victor said that she always wore her hair braided. He also said that she'd sing to us in Quechua. This was before we lived with Mima. He said that we first lived in an apartment by the church with three other women, and in the mornings, when I'd cry for milk, she'd feed me and sing, and then I'd sleep, wrapped in his old baby blanket. He remembered the blanket because it made him jealous . . . and . . . that's all I got. It's not like we'd talk about it." As Hugo spoke, he felt for his rosary, pressing the beads and feeling them crumble. Meli hardly noticed, or she pretended not to.

"Quechua?" Meli said. "Do you remember any Quechua?"

Hugo shook his head.

"One sec," Meli said. She went inside, came back out with her laptop—a real mess of a device, missing keys, cracked screen. She powered it up, navigated to YouTube, and typed in "Ketcha Bolivia Lullaby." "Do you mind?" she asked. "I want to hear what she might have sounded like."

"Sure. Go ahead," Hugo said. He finished off his beer and held her hand.

When the song played, Hugo expected something to stir in him. It's not that he wasn't moved; the song and melody were beautiful, but he didn't recognize any of it, and realizing how distant his childhood was from him then, he rested his head on

Meli's shoulder, mourning the loss of everything he'd left behind—an entire childhood forgotten or obscured. In truth, thinking about those years of his life always made him melancholic, so he preferred not to. It was something he'd practiced for so long, he came to believe, actually, that all his memories were lost, to the point that when strangers would ask him to expand on his Bolivian origin, he'd say, "I wish I could. I have this affliction. I cannot remember anything in my life before the age of nine." Most of the time, he really did believe this lie. He'd built a wall between his past and his present. He protected himself.

Hugo folded up Alexi's contract, set it aside, and opened up his web browser. He typed "Quechua," and then he let YouTube lead him down this endless "up next" of artificially curated material. He watched, intently, not because he was nostalgic and wanted to recover his youth. No. The language reminded him of Meli and the night she played the lullaby for him. Back then, he thought she was trying to figure out what kind of mother she'd be. He suspected that she was pregnant because he'd seen her standing in front of the bathroom mirror, holding her belly and pushing it out. He didn't yet know that she had no interest in being a mother. Watching her sway in the bright light of the vanity, he imagined the possibility of a family. Listening to the lullaby now, he remembered that feeling, and he wished that he'd tried harder to tell Meli what she wanted to know.

~

AT AROUND 3:45 a.m., Hugo's phone fell from his hand and smacked him in the face. When he came to, he was on the steps of

La Iglesia de San Lorenzo in Potosí. It must have been morning rush hour. School-age children hurried along the sidewalk, clustered together in cliques. Their uniforms—navy slacks, button-up shirts, and burgundy cardigans—were identical to those that he'd worn. It made Hugo nostalgic for his own schoolhouse, and for the walks that he and his brother would take each morning—exhausted because they'd worked the mines the previous night.

In Potosí, it was not uncommon for young children to earn an income this way. Some worked in the local cemetery, maintaining the altars. Others washed cars, or bused tables at small cafés or bars. But the majority of the kids worked in the mountain. Their little bodies could most easily navigate the narrow passageways, and so long as they were under fifteen, they were cheap labor.

Just then, Hugo heard a shop door slam open, and he saw two children bolt out. They ran across the street, weaving through oncoming traffic, all the way up the steps of the church, where they plunked down. One of them opened a bottle of Coca-Cola and it sprayed everywhere. The other had a box of alfajores. He was holding one to his mouth, licking off the dulce de leche that had protruded from the cookie. "Hey, Hugo! Don't lick all of them. That's gross." It was disorienting at first, but Hugo realized that he was witnessing a moment from his own childhood.

Having heard the voice of his brother—so silvery and beaming with life—he ran up the steps and said, "Victor! Victor! Is that really you?" Like before, Hugo could not engage. He was there, present but somehow absent, as if he were watching the event unfold on a movie screen.

He watched his brother shake the soda. Hugo knew this day. They'd skipped school and had taken some of their salary to buy snacks at a shop. It was the day Victor confessed that he planned on leaving for America. The mines were killing him; they were killing everyone. Victor had written to their father, asking for money to go north. He was convinced their father would come through.

"If we have the chance," he said, "we need to take it."

"But what if our mother comes back?"

"Hermano, I need you to come with me. Just imagine. We'll head north. We'll see the world, and there will be Coca-Cola everywhere. I've heard that in the United States there are entire cities that run Coca-Cola through the pipes," Victor said. "You could go to a water fountain, press the button, and drink fresh Coca-Cola right out the plumbing. Could you imagine living there?"

"You're lying. That can't be real."

Victor smiled. "Okay. Maybe not. But promise me something."

"What?"

"If our father comes through, and if he sends the money, that you'll leave with me."

"And what about Mima?"

"Don't be such a shit," Victor said. He grabbed young Hugo and squeezed.

A police officer called to them and they ran off the steps, leaving the empty bottle of Coca-Cola behind. Hugo chased them down the street and into an alley. When he crossed into the alley, smelling the filth and rot of a trash bin, he fell into a pit. At first, Hugo believed that he was back in his efficiency, in bed, but then he saw a row of lamps flicker on, and he heard people crawling through the rocky passages, dragging their drills behind them, and he knew exactly where he was.

~

OUTSIDE THE MOUNTAIN, the children belong to God. When they cry and rejoice and bask in the sunlight, they are basking in heaven. But in the mines, the children are the property of El Tío. He can be merciful. He protects those who bring him offerings, who do not cry or complain, who are productive, who will work into the twilight even if there is school the next day. It is his mountain. Miners have known this for centuries. To enter the red mountain is to enter Gehenna and to hear the king's children burning in the fires. You can hear them crying. In the mines, nothing is holy. The walls, picked at for centuries, can swallow men whole. One moment, a miner kneels to tie their laces, and the next, they're gone, digested by the stones and the darkness and the impenetrable stillness.

In the mountain, each mine has a temple for El Tío. Usually, there's a statue of his likeness covered in beads and offerings. At the totem's feet, there are plastic bottles, cigarette packs, anything. Miners begin their shift by sharing a meal with El Tío and requesting safe passage. Back when Hugo was a child worker of the mines, he and Victor would also make offerings. They didn't have much to give: a toy soldier, a weathered baseball, a bag of bones. They were committed to keeping on the good side of El Tío. When it came to sharing a meal, their choices were meager: a stick of gum, a bottle of water, a half-smoked cigar. They'd heard terrible stories from other children—children who claimed to have seen El Tío roaming the mines, eating naughty kids who'd forgotten their offerings. Victor himself swore that he'd once seen El Tío descend on a man—a ball of fire that burned right through the miner, extinguishing his life in a sudden burst of light.

So, they always prayed for safe passage through hell. And it was hell. Not the Dante's *Inferno* version. There were no Bolivian politicians being tortured. There was no tour. This hell had a colonial flair to it, a wound inflicted upon the mountain by the Spanish in the sixteenth century. In the midst of Spain's silver boom, the colonizers had enslaved the Indigenous population and used them to saturate the mountain with mercury. The mercury helped them separate silver from ore. It was a beautiful liquid, cool to the touch, and like many beautiful things, it was deadly.

As Hugo's eyes adjusted to the darkness, he could see all of it. The mountain was his history, the rickety ladders like spiders' nests upon the land, the torches in every direction. He could see the smoke rising from the mine shafts, painting the sky black, and the enslaved people dragging cartloads of mercury-soaked ore, wearing nothing at all, their dark skin bleeding and blackened by the tips of flames. He could see the enslaved people pulling out their teeth, pulling their hair, working naked because it was always so hot—a burning that wouldn't leave, even in the cool evening breeze. In his vision he could see some standing immobile, staring into nothing. Spaniards in arms enforced la mita, using lances and anything that could beat a man down. There were dead people in piles. There were piles of bones as large as the very caravels of the colonizers. Silver was loaded onto the ships—the ships that would fund the Industrial Revolution, slavery, and the world as it is known today. And though Hugo knew, from history alone, that the silver was heading to Spain, he didn't see the silver unloaded in Europe. He couldn't see Spain. What he saw was Hialeah Gardens—rows of factories and industrial shops—and there, far off in the distance, Alexi's little manicured mansion, the long driveway, the ridiculous fountain, and Alexi, the attorney himself, dressed like a Spanish king, sitting on a lawn chair, smoking a cigar, and watching his slaves build his house, one silver brick at a time. There was a statue of El Tío right there next to him, and it had sunglasses on, a short-sleeve button-up. And there was a pit in Alexi's backyard—not a pool—and when these damned souls had unloaded their hard-earned silver, they wandered into the yard like dumb little birds, flapping their arms and falling into a pit of bodies. And who was there, unloading silver at Alexi's feet? His brother, Victor, or a version of his brother—forever enslaved to the devil.

⌒

THE DAY THAT Victor died, they'd gone to see El Tío, as they often did, but Victor asked for something. He clenched Hugo's hand and said, "Tío. Help me and my brother get to America. We don't want to live this life anymore. We don't want to work in the mines anymore. We always bring you good things. Please help us." He removed his rosary and put it before the altar. How clean it had looked back then, the leather beads oiled, the crucifix still intact. "Don't give him that," Hugo said.

In another part of the mountain, dynamite blasted, making everything rumble.

"It is what I have to give, hermano."

"But it was our mother's."

"And that is why I am offering it," Victor said.

Gazing upon El Tío's stoic face, Hugo swore he'd seen the devil blink his eyes. Victor laughed off the observation; he said it was just the shadows playing tricks, but the vision scared Hugo enough that he suggested to his brother that they not work that day, and here is the tragedy: Victor didn't listen. Within an hour, while moving through the mine, Victor lost his footing. He slipped into a hole. When he slipped, he reached for a wheelbarrow, and he pulled it down over him. It seemed all the zinc in the world filled the pit that Victor had fallen into. Hugo saw miners dig. He saw miners climb down and drag his brother's body out. He saw his brother's face, ashen, its features unrecognizable. After that, he didn't see the body again until it was dressed for the funeral.

The mining cooperative paid for the event. A Mass was held at La Iglesia de San Lorenzo, though Hugo didn't sit through it. He took satisfaction in knowing that it was well attended, even if it was mostly politicians there for some photo opportunity. They must have said some nice words about labor reform. What did Hugo care? He was a child. He sat on the steps, drinking a Coca-Cola, angry. He'd only ever asked El Tío to keep him and his brother together. How he wanted to shatter that statue of El Tío—to walk into the mine with a drill and put it right to the devil's face, to drill until all of his crimson body was nothing but dust and rocks at the bottom of some shithole tunnel.

And where, he wondered, was his father—the fucking coward?

The white man who'd taken advantage of his mother and had left him and his brother to fend for themselves. Where was he!

While Hugo grieved and stewed in his anger, a stranger sat beside him. He was a tall man, with a long nose and long spindly fingers. He was well-dressed, and Hugo suspected that he was a Spaniard. The man offered him a Marlboro cigarette. Hugo declined it with a wave of his hand.

"I'm sorry to hear about your brother."

Hugo didn't respond. He wasn't in the mood for company. And why was this stranger talking to someone like him? As far as Hugo could remember, this was the first time that a white man had taken an interest in him. He thought he might be in trouble, but in grief he hardly cared.

"Hugo, my name is Santiago," the man said. He wore a crisp white shirt and black bomber jacket, a pack of cigarettes sticking out of the breast pocket. He patted Hugo's back and said, "You must be having the most horrible day." Then he pulled a letter out from behind the cigarette pack, unfolded it, and handed it to Hugo. "Your father gave this to me. Said to find you. This familiar?"

Hugo scooted away.

"Can you read?"

Hugo nodded, and he looked over the letter, recognizing Victor's penmanship.

"Now it's just us, then? On this long journey to the United States of America." When Santiago said "the United States," he smiled, almost sarcastically, and he playfully shoved Hugo.

"Señor. I don't know you," Hugo said.

Mima stepped out from the church. She greeted the Spaniard

and then whispered, "It's time." She licked her fingers and fixed Hugo's hair. "You need to say goodbye to Victor."

"Señora," Santiago said, "I need him for just a moment."

"Pues. Un segundito," she said cautiously, retreating into the ceremony.

"I want to pay my respects," Hugo said.

"Sure. Go in the church. But tomorrow, you're leaving with me."

"No. I'm not going anywhere with you," Hugo said.

"Listen!" Santiago said, holding Hugo's hand. "I'm not going to let you die like your brother. Here, take a fucking cigarette." He shoved the box of Marlboros in Hugo's face. "Take one."

Hugo didn't want to smoke, but he was afraid to say no to the Spaniard, so he took a cigarette anyway. Santiago helped him light it, and they smoked in front of the church as the parishioners sang hymns. "Sorry I yelled," Santiago said, and then they said nothing else.

When the clouds blocked out the sun and they were graced with momentary shade, Hugo looked at this stranger beside him. Santiago must have found it awkward—some young kid glaring at him while he was trying to enjoy a cigarette. Santiago made a funny face—sticking out his tongue and crossing his eyes—and Hugo laughed. It was a glimpse of a life to come, and Hugo knew that he had to leave with him. If not for a future, then to honor the wishes of his deceased brother.

BUT HE DID not know what to tell Mima, so he said nothing to her. The night before he left, he could not sleep. Before sunrise, he washed his face in a basin and then made his way to the mine to think.

The mine was still empty. With his brother's busted lamp flickering, he entered, and wound through the hollow passages until he found El Tío dormant in a cold and quiet sanctuary. There was a small boulder that Hugo used to bash in the devil's face. He kept hitting El Tío's face until there were no distinguishing features. Then he kicked the offerings, and just to spite the mountain devil, he fished through the offerings and plucked out his brother's rosary. He could feel it then, something in the room with him. But he was not afraid. El Tío, he believed, had no right to something so precious, so Hugo slid the rosary on his wrist; then he looped it around again and again until it looked like a bracelet, and he left forever. He felt brave that day, even knowing the stories about those who'd crossed El Tío. They were only stories. He'd been dumb to believe them.

Hugo walked home at sunrise. Along the way, he collected wildflowers. He had a fantasy that he would get home and find Mima awake, and that he would explain everything to her—about Santiago approaching him at the church, Victor's letter, new opportunities in the United States. He even thought that maybe Mima, upon hearing the story, would pack her bags and come along, too.

When he arrived, she was still sleeping, still in her dark funerary dress. Who was he kidding? Mima would never leave. And could she even survive such a migration to America? He could not let the Spaniard wait any longer, so he kissed her forehead and whispered goodbye. He put the flowers in a small glass bottle, took his bag, and in the soft hues of dawn left to meet Santiago.

Hugo awoke in his efficiency to the sound of birds chirping, and to the memory of his madrina clutching a pillow. He was sweating. He sat up and stumbled to the kitchen, where Meli's chair was, again, against the wall—and the catalogue he'd tossed in the trash was back on the table. Something was not right.

8

HUGO WAS NOT fully awake. On his drive to the botanica, he could feel the exhaustion in his neck. The sunrise, which made the highway and traffic radiate in those stunning South Florida flamingo hues, did not awaken his senses in the least, nor did the flock of ibises gliding above the endless rows of factories. This was Hugo's typical morning commute, a long trek up the Palmetto Expressway, past the old mall, the forward-facing wholesalers, and the many box-shaped commercial buildings.

He should have been focusing on the road, but his mind was elsewhere, back in his childhood. The dreams had awoken painful memories. Though he saw the NW 103rd Street exit sign up ahead and knew he'd have to merge onto the exit to get to work on time, he took too long to act. He checked in the side mirror. There was enough of a gap to merge safely. But traffic begets desperation, and some restless driver merged first. She accelerated at such an excessive rate that Hugo didn't even notice. When he clicked on his turning signal to cross over, cautiously, the pickup driver leaned on her horn with rage, which startled Hugo back into his lane. Then the driver, in a fit of aggression, proceeded to block Hugo from merging. It seemed spiteful. When he slowed down to merge behind her, she slowed down. When he accelerated, she also accelerated. And since she wasn't letting him into the lane, Hugo realized that he would definitely be late to work.

Cars filled the available space of the exit lane, and Hugo, turning signal still on, tried to find other cars that would show him some empathy—a semblance of early-morning humanity—but nobody even looked at him. Maybe the residents of the apartment building overlooking the expressway empathized, sipping their coffee. But every driver with a stake in getting to work on time pretended that Hugo was not there, and when it was clear that he would have to take the next exit, he lowered his windows, pulled up beside the truck, and yelled, "Thanks, asshole!"

The woman in the pickup laughed and flicked not one but two middle fingers back. Even the child in the backseat lowered her window and, from booster seat and all, flicked a middle finger. In that instant, Hugo did not see people. He saw hunks of machinery: steel and plastic and glass. He swerved toward the pickup, as if to suggest, *I'll crash into you.* How he wanted to do it, to make a stand. The woman yelled, "Nice one, you fucking Indio," so Hugo slammed on the brakes. He stuck out his middle finger as high as he could. As she exited the highway, he honked and flicked harder. The truck honked, too. And then, the ordeal was over. There was no one for Hugo to direct his anger to, so he calmed down, or he tried to. A new feeling enveloped him: the shame of being so belligerent—so spiteful. He could feel the eyes of all those early commuters on him, so he pulled ahead, and he tried to put that moment behind him. But who was he kidding? His enmity could not be displaced. It'd been there, he remembered, since the day he took the boulder and smashed the mountain devil's face, and even if he wanted to seek out peace, he knew that the anger was too enjoyable. It made him feel powerful, capable. Why pick up the pieces of his life when he could just focus his attention on something and smash it? *Yes*, he recalled. *This is why I took Alexi's case.*

HE ARRIVED AT the botanica a full thirty minutes late. There were shopping carts scattered throughout the parking lot. Before he could even park his car, he had to gather them and roll them into the grass. The sound that those carts made rattling along the pavement gave Hugo such a headache. He could feel the exhaustion spreading from his neck to behind his eyes and to the back of his skull. Worse was that the botanica's shop windows were reflecting the rising sun, so he couldn't even see Lourdes in there, judging him, likely standing with her hands on her hips. When he approached the botanica, what he saw was himself, disheveled and old-looking—not elderly but middle-aged. He hadn't remembered having such prominent bags under his eyes. There had been a time when he and Meli were young. But as the saying goes, his reflection scared his soul.

In his hand, he had Alexi's retainer money. If Lourdes started yelling, he could show her the check and calm her down. But tardiness was the one thing that set her off—apparently her sister had been late to the docks during Mariel and missed the boat.

Lourdes's employees could fail her in many immeasurable ways, but if they were late, she considered them "basura encendida," as she liked to say. In fact, the one time that Hugo had really been late to work—car trouble—she'd gotten so mad, she made him go out back and clean out each of the chicken cages, such a disgusting task. And she threatened, "You make a habit of this, Hugo, and I don't want you in the store anymore." It seemed harsh, but to her point, he'd seen Lourdes fire other employees for tardiness. Three total. And with this in mind, he pushed into the botanica, unsure which face she'd be wearing on that day, and half expecting an afternoon of cleaning dirty chicken cages.

But Lourdes was not immediately upset. She wasn't even waiting for him by the door. She was mopping the floor, dancing barefoot to Bebo Valdés's "Aquellos Ojos Verdes." All of the store smelled of citrus. It was cleansing in ways that made Hugo feel more awake, energized. There was a sense of cheerfulness in the botanica, too. Lourdes was in her cleaning lady getup, and she looked so ridiculous in it. The outfit always made Hugo smile. Along the counter, she'd put up a string of holiday lights, taped to the glass display. "Buenos días, jefa. Can I help you with that?"

"¡Oye! The floor is wet," she shouted, leaning on her mop and pointing. "Don't you come in with your dirty feet. You stand there," she said, while continuing to pass the mop around. This was odd, Hugo thought. Usually, he was the one that mopped. Not to mention he didn't know what cleaning product she was using. He'd always used Fabuloso. But this citrus scent, it was new, and beneath its astringent scent, he could detect something else, traces of cigar smoke.

"Lourdes, did you have a party or something?"

"No," she said. "No. I didn't. And if I had a party and didn't invite you, what's that to you? Why do I have to invite you to everything?" She smiled when she said this, clearly teasing him, and then she said, "Don't think I don't see what's going on here. You're late, Hugo! You know better."

He was still at the threshold, the door wide open. He could feel the sun on his back, and the store's A/C escaping past him. While he was standing there, blocking the entrance, a woman tapped him on the shoulder as if to enter. "Hola, chica!" Lourdes shouted. "How are you? Mira. Just give me a sec. El piso está mojado." So, the woman stood there with Hugo, and after a few minutes, someone else appeared, and then another person, and by 9:15 a.m., there was a line forming, and the floor was still glistening. "Tell them it'll be five minutes, Hugo," Lourdes shouted, so he did, but that wasn't enough for the crowd. One man walked away, frustrated. A young woman who'd been looking down at her phone the whole time sucked on her teeth and said, "Unbelievable, bro! I got to come back after work." When ten minutes had passed, a patron asked, "Can we come in now?" Lourdes, who was sitting on a stool watching the floor dry, said, "Not yet." At that point, all the patrons left. Some would be back, for sure, but Hugo knew that this was no way to run a business. And when the last of the patrons were gone, Lourdes seemed relieved. "How'd it go with the attorney?"

"Good," Hugo said. "I have the retainer, and I'm scheduled to see Alexi again tonight."

Lourdes nodded. "And will he hold up his end of the cigar? Will he cancel your debt?"

"I have it in writing," he said, pulling out the contract and unfolding it.

Lourdes nodded. Then she got up off the stool and walked over to Hugo, careful to step only on the dried sections of the floor. She took the contract, read through it. Her reaction was unexpected. She looked upset, and Hugo worried that he'd done something to offend her. Or, worse, that Lourdes was regretting her benevolence, and that she would want some form of compensation if Alexi wrote off his debt. It was just a thought—a seed of malcontent. Lourdes had never, as far as Hugo had seen, ever made a fuss about her finances, but still, he couldn't square away this lingering feeling, like maybe she wanted more of a cut. "I need to tell you something," she said. "And I don't want you to take this the wrong way. But I don't think you should go tonight."

"What? Why would you say that?"

"Because, Hugo, I have a really bad feeling about this haunting."

"A feeling?"

"Mira, Hugo. I know you don't believe in this—"

"So, let me guess. You want to take over the case?"

Lourdes nodded. "First of all," she said, "when I'm speaking, you let me finish what I'm saying. I'm not some chick off the street, okay? And yes. I think I should be the point of contact."

"You want the money, huh?"

"Hugo! Don't be such a comemierda."

What Hugo did next was highly uncharacteristic of him. Maybe it was some of that residual anger, left over from the traffic incident, or maybe Hugo was just tired of being in debt. In any case, he stepped into the store, dirty shoes and all, and he walked right over to the register and set the retainer down. Actually, he didn't set it down at all. Because when he entered the store, his heart rate increased, and he started breathing heavily. Lourdes said, "El piso!" But Hugo didn't care, and, in fact, he rubbed the soles of his shoes against the floor just to spite her, and he took that envelope, lifted it way over his head, and slammed it down on the counter, and as he did this, he could feel his enmity hardening in his chest and spreading through his body and then out of his body and onto the floor and the shelves and even onto Lourdes herself—an enmity that seemed to blanket the whole world. And seeing how all of the store was painted by his rage, he said, "¡Métetelo en el culo!" And upon insulting her, he felt something else. He felt, in him, a desire to insult her more, to bury her with profanity. He could feel this wrath, all the ways in which he was losing control—the quivering of his leg, his exasperated breathing. And Lourdes, who was on the receiving end of his insult, took the money, held it up, and said, "Oh, really! What did you want me to do with this again?"

But before Hugo could respond, she laughed. She laughed so hard, it made Hugo feel less tense. "Hugo!" she said, "I've never heard you use that language," which was true. He never had. Why now? And when he was calm and apologetic, she said, "I'm not the bad person here. And I'm not going to shove this up my ass." She laughed. "Come here, my Bolivian friend." She took his hands, rubbed citrus oil onto them. "Try to relax, okay."

He took a deep breath.

"Tell me, what got into you?"

"It's just, I'm so close to being free of it. I need this, Lourdes."

"And?"

"I'm sorry I spoke to you that way. But I need to see this through."

"I understand that," she said, releasing his hands. A patron walked in, proceeded to browse. "But I have to warn you," Lourdes continued. "This haunting is a little different. You're used to small things, Hugo. And there's a reason this attorney is so desperate. You must know that."

"Excuse me," the patron said. "Do you have any—"

"Don't you hear me in the middle of something?" Lourdes shouted, and just like that, the patron left the store. But Lourdes didn't seem to care. She locked the front door, then took Hugo's hand again and said, "Listen. Listen to me. I had a vision last night. I was at the botanica late at night, except it looked different. The shelves were gone, and in the center, there was a white stone." Here, Lourdes paused like this was supposed to mean something to Hugo. He was utterly perplexed.

"On the stone," she said, "there was a devil smoking a cigar, looking for you."

At this, Hugo was surprised.

"Ah . . . Yes. There it is. You know this devil, don't you?"

"Please," Hugo said. "Finish the story."

"His skin was red. He wore thousands of beaded necklaces, and on his head, there were horns. I've never had a vision like that, Hugo. And you know what the devil wanted? You won't believe me, but the devil said, 'Tell me, Lourdes. How do I become an attorney in the US?'"

"Now you're joking with me," Hugo said.

"No. He came to me for advice. What do I know about becoming an attorney!"

"What did you tell him?"

"I don't help devils. I told him that."

"I don't believe you."

"Why would a devil be looking for you?" Lourdes asked.

"Well," Hugo said. "Dreams don't always have to be omens."

"Ay, Hugo! You know it means something."

"I've got a headache, okay," Hugo said.

"He mentioned that you're indebted to him."

"So he's Alexi then. That explains it, no?"

"Fine. You want to keep secrets. Fine!"

"If you don't mind, we should open up already. Or do you intend to turn away all of our customers?" Hugo opened the storefront himself, waved a patron in, and proceeded to work as if nothing had happened. But now he was scared. How would Lourdes have known? It didn't make any sense, and frankly, Hugo didn't have the mental space for such thoughts. What he wanted, simply, was to finish the Alexi case. So he told Lourdes nothing of his dream or of El Tío. Her vision, poignant as it was, was eclipsed by his remorse. He regretted his anger, and he dwelled on it.

BACK WHEN MELI was recovering from her surgery, she hadn't been eating well. Hugo was worried about her, but he was also worried about his finances and a bit overwhelmed by all the cleaning and the blood and the administering of her postsurgical care. Even though Lourdes had given him time off to care for Meli, it didn't feel like time off. He'd gone from one hectic job to another job, and it was a lot for Hugo. Sure, there were days when some of Meli's friends would bring over casseroles or pots filled with rice and beans, and this helped—except she was hardly eating. Anytime Hugo brought her a bowl of something healthy, she'd just sit in bed, spoon in hand, paralyzed by the TV.

So, Hugo decided he'd make her chicken soup. Where this desire came from, who knows? It wasn't as if chicken noodle soup was a staple of his diet. When he was young, and coming down with the flu, it wasn't as if Santiago had ever made him a pot of soup. Hugo had probably come to associate soup with healing from television. Memories of Joey from *Friends* sitting across the table from a young child, botching his lines in a commercial, made him laugh. "'Soup. I mean, noodle soup,'" he recited. Meli, who loved *Friends* probably above all shows, would adore the joke. And, more importantly, she'd have a decent meal and feel much better.

But making chicken noodle soup from scratch was a commitment. First, he made a trip to the grocer, but those chickens were way too expensive. *Why pay top dollar for a chicken*, he thought, *when I could get one at the botanica, fresh?* So that's what he did. Lourdes thought his plan was so crazy, she gave him the chicken outright and said, "These aren't really for eating, but I guess you can. Where are you going to put it? Do you have a cage?" He didn't, so he took it in his hands. Clearly, Hugo hadn't thought his plan through. He knew that almost immediately when, while he tried to navigate the Palmetto Expressway, his soon-to-be dinner kept clucking and flapping its wings wildly from the backseat to the front seat, leaving feathers floating everywhere. He should have put it in the trunk. Oh well, he thought. Next time. There was also the issue of killing the chicken. This he had done many times with clients, and he usually committed the act with gardening shears. It sounded violent, sure, but Hugo had grown quite skilled at applying just the right amount of force. He didn't want the chicken's head to come off partially. It had to be humane. Typically, the customer would hold the chicken steady, and Hugo would sever the head. It was really, in his mind, a two-person operation. Since he couldn't, in good conscience, ask Meli to do the job, he decided to try it out himself, chasing the chicken around the side yard with open shears. This did not work. Frustrated and brimming with a new idea, Hugo proceeded to lay the chicken's head down on a piece of stone and to use another stone to bash its head in. This, he thought, would surely kill the chicken, only it didn't. It made things worse. Maybe he hadn't struck the chicken hard enough. Now the chicken was running around the side yard all funny-looking, with crap oozing out of its eyes, and it was really beginning to make noise. *When in doubt*, Hugo thought, *YouTube*. He wished he'd gone online sooner. In one video, a man held a chicken by the head until it was relaxed and "asleep," and then he snapped its neck with a sudden violent gesture. Hugo tried it, and it worked right away! He was so pleased with the instructional video, he left a comment below: "Best chicken killing video!"

Now there was the business of defeathering and cleaning the chicken, at which point Hugo began to wonder whether he should have, in fact, just purchased a chicken whole. Was all this work worth a $15.48 savings? The video suggested he boil a pot of hot water before plucking, so he did. He left the dead chicken out on a stone, got the pot boiling nicely. "Babe, what are you up to?" Meli shouted from the bedroom. Hugo smiled. "Just prepping dinner, my love." He was so excited to finally be cooking something of substance for her. When he carried the pot of hot water out into the yard, he was shocked to see a cat pawing at the dead chicken, biting into it. He dropped the pot, nearly searing himself, and chased the cat away. "Fucking cat!" But after a short inspection, he concluded that the cat hadn't really done too much damage. It had only chewed on the chicken's gut. So, he continued with his plan, dunking the chicken into the pot for a few seconds, at least, then pulling it out to defeather. The pot was quite small, so Hugo did the best he could.

The cat watched the whole time.

The feathers came out quite easily. Hugo then took the giblets and the innards and tossed them for the cat, feeling quite accomplished. The cat was thrilled, its tail high up in the air. And Hugo watched the creature devour the intestines and heart. By then, he'd been working on this project for at least an hour, and so it was time to get the soup ready. He chopped up the ingredients, following a recipe by some gringa named Rachael Ray, who seemed nice enough, and after four hours of work, the soup was ready. Not only was it ready, it smelled amazing. The broth alone would be enough to revitalize Meli; it would go straight to her bones. And he was especially proud because he'd found a reason to use the dill in his herb garden.

When he offered it to Meli, who was in bed watching television, she took a sip and set the soup down. She didn't say "thank you." She didn't comment on the flavor of the soup. She was so enraptured by the television, she hardly noticed. And Hugo, disappointed by this reaction, stepped into the kitchen. He tried not to think too much of it. She was sick, after all. So, he washed the dishes, and as he was doing this, he glanced around the efficiency.

Meli had left her clothing on the floor by the bedroom; it'd been there for days. There were catalogues open and splayed all over their table. The garbage was overflowing. Out back, there was still a dirty pot, bloody garden shears, and a bag filled with bloody feathers and chicken feet and, if the cat hadn't gotten to it, a chicken neck and head. Hugo felt dirty. He was so tired. A tight ball of resentment formed inside him. It was surprising at first—to resent her so strongly. And he thought, *Calm down. Just tell her how you feel.* So he walked into the bedroom and said, "You're not even going to say anything?" She was a bit taken aback by his bluntness, and she said, "Oh. It's really great, babe. Really." But that didn't make Hugo feel any better. He was angry. And in that moment, in the midst of having done something kind for his wife, Hugo said, "I am beginning to resent you."

Meli paused the television, and she looked over at Hugo, bewildered. With more time, she might have asked, "Why would you say that?" But she didn't respond. She seemed shocked. And Hugo, knowing that he'd crossed a line—that he had said something hurtful and reprehensible—doubled down: "I don't know if I can do this *thing* anymore."

"I'm a little confused," she said.

"Of course you are."

"What is that supposed to mean?" Meli asked.

"Enough," he yelled. "I've got things to do."

"No! What you said . . . I hope you're not saying that you want to leave me?"

That was not what Hugo had meant, but he said, "You're just like your family, you know?"

"Yeah! And how exactly?"

"Ungrateful. Snobbish. You expect the world to cater to you."

"You're being mean," she said. "I just had surgery."

"It's always something, huh?"

Meli cried, and though Hugo knew he should stop his tirade immediately, he could not. His enmity had taken hold of him. She took the cup of soup in her hands and sipped and said, "I really do appreciate you, Hugo. You know that. I just can't believe what you said. Do you mean that?"

"Well? Do you like it or what?"

"Are we still talking about the soup?"

"I do everything around here. Everything!" he shouted, and he grabbed her clothing off the floor, balled it up, and threw it at her. "Would it hurt," he said, "to pick up after yourself?"

"Actually, yes. It would, asshole. Or did you forget? I had surgery!"

And after that comment, Hugo proceeded to shout and toss things around, making more of a mess the whole time. He went so far as taking all of the chicken soup he'd made and pouring it down the drain. In doing so, he'd failed to sift the bits of chicken and bone and noodles out, and because they didn't have a garbage disposal, he clogged the sink. He had to dig this all out of the sink with his hands, and the futility of so much effort—of having wasted a chicken—enraged him.

Hugo was so upset, he packed a bag and threatened to leave, and at this phase of the argument, Meli, who'd just had surgery, actually stood, against doctor's orders, and came to Hugo, and she pleaded, "Please don't be like this. Please, Hugo. You're making this so much worse." And seeing Meli in such pain, crying, Hugo's enmity dissolved, and he sat on a dining chair gazing about at all the damage that he'd done—to their home and to their relationship. "Jesus Christ," he said.

"Okay, Hugo. Okay. Just come to bed with me. Just lie with me."

"But I have to clean up the mess . . . the feathers and shit."

"The what? What are you talking about? Just come to bed, okay?"

So, he did. The cat could have all the scraps, he thought. In bed, he held her, feeling such grief at how everything had transpired. Why had he been so angry? He didn't know. *Things were supposed to be nice today.* He promised her that he'd never act that way again, and he worried that he'd broken something irreplaceable in their relationship. He held her, and he prayed that they would always be together. He prayed that she could forgive him. When she died, three weeks later, he couldn't help but wonder whether his shouting episode had contributed to her complications. He had no way of knowing. What he knew was that he hated the monster in him—that unquenchable anger. And having forgotten about the bag of feathers, it was only after her funeral that he found it all: the decomposing chicken head, and the feathers scattered about his small side yard. And shortly after that grim discovery, Hugo sat at his table, sorted through his mail, and found Alexi's letter. "Collect," it had said. "But she's dead," Hugo had whispered, and he whispered it again and again until he could feel the knot of enmity in his chest like a loaded gun looking for someone to point at.

9

AFTER WORK, HUGO had an hour to kill before his meeting with Alexi. He veered off the major streets and drove through the quiet residential neighborhoods, which resembled small and unmanaged parking lots—cars atop sidewalks and grass, cars squeezed tightly into their spaces, glistening and new. Two days until Christmas Eve. South Florida was in lights, and Hugo wanted to resent it.

The festivities reminded him of Meli, the way she fetishized the snow—how every year after Thanksgiving, she'd go so far as spraying snow-colored paint and glitter on the insides of their windows. He thought it a waste, at $5 per can, but since she'd never seen snow, and because she so desperately wanted a white Christmas, Hugo didn't make a big deal out of it, nor did he dampen her mood with stories of his own winters shoveling snow, feeling the cold slice through his mittens.

This dream of a snowy South Florida—of children ice-skating

on a frozen swamp and icicles hanging from palm fronds and al-
ligators wearing Santa hats—intrigued Hugo very much, and
he found that ever since he'd lost Meli, he, too, longed for a
white Christmas. This time of the year, whenever Hugo thought
about snow, he'd recall Meli in her pajamas, sitting by the window on Christmas Eve, the way she'd look up at the storm clouds
and check her weather app and say, "It could happen. Could you
imagine, Hugo, if it really snowed in Miami? That would be
amazing!"

"Meli," he'd say. "It'd be a disaster. Who would salt the roads?
Shovel the walks?"

But it would be nice. Although Hugo had been in a sour mood
all day, something about driving through town and seeing entire
neighborhoods brimming with decorations lifted his spirits. How
touching it was to see children outside, buzzing with joy as they
helped their parents string lights on palm trees. Sometimes Hugo
would stop at a traffic light, and there beside him, shining through
someone's window, he'd see a Christmas tree. Hugo wanted to
celebrate the holiday, too, a tree by the window, the glow from
within the pine needles. Maybe this Christmas he'd bring out
Meli's old decorations: the light-up snowman that they'd bought
at CVS; the Christmas cards they'd written to each other throughout the years; the red candles and the Santa-themed candlehold-
ers that Meli had inherited from her mother. He went as far as
checking his wallet to see if he had enough to buy cans of spray
snow. As Hugo lost himself in these fantasies, he found that in his
meanderings, he'd cruised all the way to Hialeah Gardens, a mere
few blocks from Alexi's haunted mansion.

~

DURING HIS LAST visit, Hugo hadn't fully appreciated Alexi's Christmas extravagance; the outdoor decorations hadn't been plugged in. But now, as he pulled into his driveway, it was impossible to look away. For starters, there was a life-size Nativity off the western corner of the lot, and not of the inflatable variety. Passersby could, aptly, look through Alexi's iron fence and see Baby Jesus in the manger. The columns of Alexi's house were wrapped in stringed white lights and from the ceiling hung icicle lights, which flicked on and off in ways that made them seem like they were dripping down. Inflatable Mickey and Minnie were caroling under a lamppost, alongside Scrooge McDuck. The place oozed Christmas, down to the snowflakes that were being projected on the wall.

Hugo, who'd been entranced by the quaint decorations in other neighborhoods, now felt offended by Alexi's display. "Se tiró el pedo más alto," Lourdes would say, and it was true. Even his "All Lives Matter" sign had a tasteful display of blue Christmas lights around its borders.

Touring the driveway, Hugo didn't know what offended him exactly, or why. He'd never seen an inflatable Christmas decoration that was asking to get punched in the face. The mansion appeared to him, just as it had appeared in his nightmares, made of silver. The whole house looked coated in it. And how could Hugo gaze upon such grandeur and not think of his homeland? This was the problem with the world, he reasoned, people like Alexi hoarding wealth, and for *this*?

Again, Hugo, who was not *really* a babaláwo, did not even attempt to seek out the demonic vibrations of the house. Having been in the car for quite some time, he stretched his arms and fingers, and he smacked his lips, tasting the familiar metallic tinge of the industrial sector nearby. *What's my angle here?* he thought, popping his trunk and browsing through his "tools of the trade": a bag of white sage for smudging, accompanied by an abalone shell and a peacock feather; an all-seeing eye amulet; a vial of holy water, a vial for the orishas; sulfur powder; a dozen or so evil eye bracelets (for distributing); a small bag of chicken bones; devotionals specifically dedicated to casting away evil; a bulk-sized container of pink salt; a cigar lighter; and vesta powder (for effect).

In the eyes of his customers, such artifacts might seem imbued with supernatural powers, but Hugo knew better. He was the one who'd unbox them in the botanica's warehouse. He was the one who checked to see that the shipment matched the order, and he was the one to stock and take inventory. These strange little objects were not made in some santero's sanctuary; they were made in China. If supplies ran low, Lourdes could easily place another order online, and voilà: more product.

But Hugo also knew the allure of such artifacts. When Meli was sick, he also turned to them. Something about lighting a healing candle made him feel like he had control. Not that it mattered. Death took Meli anyway, and in the end, all the botanica shit went into the trash, probably into that giant mountain of trash looming over and away from Alexi's property. Still, Hugo knew of the lasting power of a sacred object, which was why he always used at least one object from his stash. This evening, he decided he'd distribute the evil eye bracelets, one for each family member.

But the evil eye bracelets would not be enough. Hugo needed to figure out a way to make Alexi *believe* that the haunting was under control. Seeing all the Christmas lights, the excess of it all, Hugo suddenly knew what he needed to do. The lights! Of course. The lights! They were not just about Christmas. They were also Alexi's way of honoring his parents, of showing them that their exile from Cuba had been worth it because now Alexi could live a life better than theirs—to have the freedom to decorate. The lights! They were his affirmation of all that was possible in America.

Hugo suspected that this haunting in Hialeah Gardens was nothing more than some second-generation Cuban American attorney trying to deal with a moral failing. That's why he'd seen Rocio, the first woman he'd ever collected on. Of course! It made sense. Just as Alexi was moving into his dream home—just as he was actualizing one of his life goals—he realized that he'd hurt people along the way, people like Rocio, who'd had her wages garnished up until her death. *Yes! Yes!* Hugo thought. *This can work.* So, what Hugo needed to do was fully awaken this moral conflict in Alexi—make the price of Alexi's work so painful that it would break him. And then, and only then, could Hugo help him heal. How would he do that? By helping him believe that his work was noble, that the people he collected on were deserving of their financial ruin. Alexi would need to think of them as fish in a pond. Not even fish. Worms, waiting to be baited. It was a strange realization: In order to help Alexi, and thereby clear his debt, Hugo would have to teach Alexi to never feel any remorse toward a debtor again. He would need to cast not the demon out from the house but the human out from the debtor, thereby returning the debtor to nothing but a mere number on a report.

~

ALEXI MUST HAVE noticed Hugo stalking the property. The giant McMansion door swung open, and as the attorney fumbled out, dressed in the same exact outfit as the day before, his daughter made a beeline for the flurry of Christmas lights. Little Dulce was already in her Disney Princess nightgown, which was so long it dragged on the ground. "Hey, Hugo!" she yelled, and then she danced in the projector's snowflakes, barefoot.

"To be a child," Alexi said, shaking Hugo's hand. "Blessed."

"I almost didn't recognize the place," Hugo said. "You like Christmas, huh?"

"Who doesn't?" Alexi said, beaming with pride. "It's my favorite time of the year."

"Me, too!" Dulce shouted. "Christmas lights! Christmas lights!" And as she repeated this refrain again and again, Alexi knelt beside her and whispered something into her ear, at which point she said, "Good night," and she ran inside. Hugo and Alexi followed. "I like being able to do this, you know?" Alexi said, closing the door behind Hugo. "My parents never did decorate much."

"Oh, really?"

"Yeah. When you come from Cuba with nothing, splurging on decorations doesn't seem that sensible. I'm not complaining," he said. "They made good financial choices. This is proof, no?"

"It's a lot of decorations. Good for you!" Hugo said. "We should get started, no?"

But Alexi didn't budge beyond the foyer. It was especially awkward because Hugo, who'd come to feel quite welcome at the Ramirez residence, now felt out of sorts. In truth, he'd expected to be invited to dinner once more. "Are you all right?" Hugo asked. "Did something else happen?"

"I want to talk about yesterday," Alexi said, shifting his weight from one leg to the other. It was probably the way he behaved in court, fidgeting with his hands and the buttons on his shirt. "Because I've been thinking about it," he said. "I've been thinking, specifically, about the hex bag."

Hugo had an idea where the conversation was going. Alexi was having his doubts. This kind of thing happened sometimes. Clients would get cold feet. When he mentioned the hex bag, he'd paused as if waiting for Hugo to reveal something incriminating, but Hugo, who was not new to his line of business, knew just how to respond. "It's a wanga bag. Not a hex bag. Wanga. *W-a-n-g-a.*"

"Sorry. What was that?"

"You said hex bag, but what we found was a wanga bag."

"Yes," he said. "Well, I've been thinking. We'd just recently planted those ferns."

"Okay."

"No. You don't understand. We did. Claudia and Dulce did the job themselves."

"A nice family activity."

"It was," Alexi said. "So, you can see why I might be a bit suspicious about yesterday's events."

"How so? Please," Hugo said. "Tell me what's on your mind."

"That neither me, nor Claudia, nor Dulce planted that hex bag . . . wanga thing there."

"I would hope not," Hugo said, smiling. "Why would you?" And after a moment of uncomfortable silence, Hugo said, "Oh. Oh. I see. Are you accusing me of planting the bag?"

"Look. I'm just asking," Alexi said.

"Your theory about Haitians doesn't pan out, so it has to be me now?"

"Claudia thinks the whole thing was crazy. She doesn't believe you're the real deal."

"I know it can be shocking for those who do not believe."

"You know, she got a call from Emily and the kids down the street about me urinating. It's embarrassing. And now, I'm wondering: Is any of this legit?"

"I'm disappointed by this," Hugo said. "You are the one that called me. Even with my reservations, I came here to help you and your family. I'm here tonight. If you don't want help . . ."

"Okay. Okay," Alexi said, now hanging his head low. "But who could have done it?"

"You want the answer, but I don't have it yet."

"If it wasn't the Haitians, then who?"

"I don't know, my friend," Hugo said, shaking his hand. "Do you know anyone who might know what a wanga bag is?"

"No. Nobody."

"Who recommended our botanica to you?"

"My employee Gloria. But no way!"

"Who?"

"Gloria. She's one of my longtime employees. But she's practically family."

"Then I doubt it's her," Hugo said. "Now shouldn't we find a place to sit? If we're to find out what's behind these strange occurrences of yours, I'll need to learn more."

"I'd like to know who planted that bag there," Alexi said. "Who does something like that?"

"Well," Hugo said, smiling. "Usually, it's somebody you've wronged. But we'll get to that." And with those words, he walked past Alexi, seizing control of the conversation once again.

HUGO WOULDN'T HAVE admitted it, but he was excited to tour more of Alexi's property. Judging by the great pool area and the regal entranceway, he suspected the rest of Alexi's home to be quite luxurious, the stuff that Meli would have gone wild over. But walking through the Florida room and into the living room was such a letdown. Clearly, money could not buy style. Something had gone awry in the interior decorating—a battle waged between modern aesthetics and neoclassical ones. It felt, to Hugo, as if he were walking through an IKEA showroom. The sheer size of the rooms made the home *really* feel more like those zoo enclosures than a place to raise a family. But to be certain, there was some warmth: a grandiose Christmas tree standing tall in the Florida room, decked out with white lights and hundreds of silver and golden ornaments. It was a tree dressed for adults, not for Dulce. There were no cartoon characters. No bright colors. No train beneath it. It was likely that Alexi had plucked the thing out of a catalogue, ready-made, and upon closer inspection, Hugo confirmed that he had. It was a fake tree. Of course it would be in a home such as this.

Their living room? Inexcusable. What a cold, cold place, exacerbated by the high ceilings and the dirty oversized fish tank. Hugo could see, just glancing, a small shark circling the tank. Such a cruel thing to do. Alexi had probably purchased it to make a statement about his character, and lo and behold, when they passed the tank, he tapped the glass and said, "See the shark." Such a child.

A low, oversized white leather sectional served as the living room's dominant piece of furniture. It had metal pegs for legs, as if he'd assembled the thing himself out of a box. And the sectional was having an identity crisis. Was it sleek and modern, as its general frame suggested, or was it baroque, as the silver-studded and curved armrests implied? It did not look comfortable in the least. It lay atop a rose-colored shag rug. For a coffee table, they had an equally oversized ottoman, also white. And on the ottoman, a silver-colored tray and silver pieces of brain coral as decor.

"Do you sense anything today?" Alexi asked, gesturing to his sitting area. "Any spirits?"

The only supernatural thing that Hugo felt, walking through the residence, was how the furnishings and decor seemed to pull the warmth and soul right out of him. The house was vacuous. Hugo could even hear his footsteps echoing far off in its empty travertine extremities. So fake. Hugo felt as if he were inside the idea of a home and not a home itself. Even the walls, not just white but flat, matte, a cheap coat. It looked like chalk. And on the walls, there were those tacky Cuban paintings that people hawk at festivals. To Hugo's right, a painting of a green lizard, its strawberry-like dewlap fully extended—yes, lizards! To his left, a wheelbarrow filled with mangoes, a beach, palms—of course, the rustic Cuban painting. And in front of him, a supersized portrait of a young Elián González, framed by clouds, where apparently his mother and some dolphins smiled down from heaven. Clearly, Alexi was one of *those* Cubans. He wasn't an exile himself, but his parents were, and Alexi had come to understand his cubanidad by embracing their exile at an emotional level, devoid of important historical context. This was the case with so many of the privileged Cubans. Hugo was so offended by Alexi's art, he thought: *Look no further! You take everyone's money, then you use it to decorate your house like this! Case solved! You're haunted by your unforgivable bad taste.*

Perhaps all of the world's problems could be reduced to this: the way Alexi could take such pride in his decor, oblivious to Hugo's offended sensibilities. If people could not even agree on the things that make a house aesthetically pleasing, then what hope could there be? The artifacts that inhabited Alexi's home seemed, to Hugo, nothing more than cultural capital. Did Alexi really like sharks? Had Elián left such a profound impact on Alexi's life to warrant such a large portrait? Or were these things—all these things—just a way for Alexi to show off his place in his community?

"Nice paintings," Hugo said, approaching the collection as if at a museum.

"Thanks!" Alexi said. "You really like them?"

"Yes. They're . . . so colorful."

"A lot of people don't know, but I painted them myself." And watching him approach the green anole, to gaze at the strokes up close, the paint lumps carelessly spread, littered here and there with parts of a brush that had molted off, Hugo felt sorry for him. He wondered how a man like Alexi could ever make time to paint. Between his firm and his family, he'd managed to keep the dream alive, and realizing this made Hugo hate him that much less. Yes! In some parallel universe, Alexi could have been a painter, selling his atrocities at local festivals, not hounding debt.

How sad that the only truly lived-in element of the living room was a small Rapunzel Disney Princess sprawled out on the sectional, her face scribbled black by crayons, her hair now coarse. Hugo reached out to touch the little doll, but Alexi grabbed it, apologized for his daughter's "insufferable" mess, and tossed it aside, at some wicker basket filled with her toys. "Let's sit."

"Yes. Of course," Hugo said, sitting on the aggressively stiff couch. *Is this a couch of rocks?* Alexi sat as well, kicking his legs up on the sectional and really getting comfortable. It was at this stage that Hugo removed his satchel, laid it on the sectional. "Do you mind?" he asked. Alexi kicked his legs off and leaned in, just as Hugo revealed the contents of his bag. Hugo set a few items on the little metal tray: a candle, a vial of water, his lighter, and the bracelets. Hugo also gathered his notebook and a blue pen, to keep an account of their conversation. He then, sensing Alexi's curiosity fully piqued, closed the bag and set it by his own feet and well out of sight. "I'd like to—"

"Wait," Alexi said. "Do you plan on burning the candle on the tray? One sec." He retrieved a porcelain coaster and set the candle atop. "Claudia would kill me if the tray got ruined."

"It's perfectly fine," Hugo said, lighting the candle. "Let us begin then. This candle is for the orisha Elegua, who is the orisha of caminos, roads, and who we honor here today. Elegua will protect us, in the span of our conversation, from evil. Let us invite this protection." At this point, Hugo closed his eyes and recited a prayer: "To you, Elegua, please keep this evil away from this man and his family. Protect them when they are awake and when they are asleep. Accept my prayer. And please bless this man, his family, his home, and our work casting out evil."

"Yes," Alexi said. "Amen. Thank you."

Hugo then took the evil eye bracelets, held them to the candle, and sprinkled them with holy water. Some of the water also blessed the travertine. Alexi quickly cleaned it with his socks. "And these," Hugo said, "are bracelets that will protect their bearers from evil. I have three here."

Alexi accepted them, chuckling. "Well. Not sure it's Claudia's style, but thank you."

"So now," Hugo said, making the sign of the cross, "let us begin. Tell us, Alexi, about some of the encounters you've had in this house. This will help me understand how to proceed in this cleansing. I need to know about these encounters and, especially, how they've made you feel."

"One second. You said 'us' just a moment ago. 'Tell us.'"

"Tonight you are speaking to Elegua through me."

"Got it! God. Where should I begin? Do we really have to get into it? Can't you just perform a ritual or something? I know you have sage. Wouldn't a smudging be fine? The sooner, the better."

"No. This is not a transaction, Alexi. You cannot order a cleansing on Amazon." Hugo chuckled. "Well, maybe you can. What you need to understand is: We're embarking on a process."

"That's fine," Alexi said. "I'm just so tired of it. I'll tell you anything you want to know."

"Well then," Hugo said, preparing his notepad. "Begin here: What has scared you most?"

UNDER DIFFERENT CIRCUMSTANCES, Hugo thought he could have been a writer. Well, maybe not a novelist, though he certainly had a lively way of taking notes. He knew how to choose just the right details, just the right words—the kinds of words that could really make a report come alive. And the words he loved most were the ones that seemed, almost, as if they didn't appertain. Maybe it was Santiago's influence and Hugo's own sense of dislocation. Who knows? In those months when he and Hugo were adjusting to a new life in the United States, it was stories that grounded him most. There was a story, it turned out, for just about anything. If Hugo spotted frogs near the ponds in the apartment community, there was a story about them. If Hugo wet the bed, or struggled to make new friends, or didn't want to eat his food or clean his room, there were stories for that. So, when Hugo asked about his mother and father, Santiago had a story about that, too. It was a bedtime story. And in that story, there was a young boy who lived alone in the desert, and who did not know why his parents had left him there. To make matters worse, they'd left him with only a silver shovel. What was he to do? He dug, and he dug, and after many years, he decided *enough is enough is enough!* And he went in search of his parents. He traveled the whole world, on a quest to show every single person his

shovel, and to ask: *Are you my mother? My father?* And the boy suc-
ceeded in his quest—he spoke not only to every human, but to
every animal, and every creature—but he still did not have any
answers. So, when he was done, he returned to his desert and sat
on a small rock, and he leaned on his shovel and cried. Because,
at worst, his parents were dead. At best, he'd met them, and they
had lied to him—forsaken him. So, the boy cried, and his tears
turned the desert sands into clay, and the desert animals, so annoyed by his incessant whining and grieving, built a wall out of
the clay and closed him off. But this, too, wasn't enough. Because
the animals could still hear him crying. So, they rolled over rocks,
poured sand and ore all over him, so much, until there was an
entire mountain where he'd once sat crying, so that when his
parents, one day, did return to claim him and apologize, they
couldn't find him. Or maybe, in those days of Hugo's youth, this
was how he remembered the story.

~

ALEXI EXPLAINED THAT on the night of the haunting,
Claudia had fallen asleep while reading to Dulce, and although
Alexi did not mention it, Hugo understood that he might have
been frustrated—home and with no prospect of a little after-hours
action. So, Alexi spread out in the living room, a bowl of already
pitted cherries on his lap and a glass of scotch in hand (not that it
matters, but Alexi stated, for the record, that he'd purchased the
cherries because he'd read, in a men's magazine, they paired nicely
with scotch—and had "Seven Health Boosts You Wouldn't Even
Believe"). He was in his pajamas—a discolored plain Hanes

T-shirt and some argyle drawstring pants—his legs sore from sitting for so many hours, driving from one backwoods Florida courthouse to another. "Backwoods" was the unfortunate term that Alexi had used, clearly exerting his dominance. Yes! Even when he discussed his hauntings, Alexi imagined himself to be better than others. Hugo was keenly aware of this posturing, and he made an account of Alexi's supremacy on the notepad.

Friday night, the family in bed, Alexi was resigned to just "chill," so he picked up his favorite book, a memoir (though he referred to it as a novel) that he claimed to have read at least five times. The book was dog-eared and marked up enough that Hugo understood Alexi's claim to be true. It was none other than Carlos Eire's *Waiting for Snow in Havana*, which is unforgivable garbage. Hugo knew this book. It's Cuban nostalgia porn. He'd been forced to read it in a high school literature class. His teacher, an exile herself, had found Eire's account so riveting, especially the lizards, and she really latched onto the Q&A at the back of the book—to the way that Eire so boldly proclaimed that English is the language of *our* country. What a douchebag. To Hugo, the whole book was just another example of some Cuban Americans thinking they're the best thing to have happened to Latin America since the United States. And it is terrible, objectively speaking. There's a whole chapter on the number thirteen. Who cares? "Masturbatory" is what came to mind. Apparently the dude was a professor of history, probably some diversity hire, making coladas for all the americanos. In any case, that was the book, and, to make matters worse, Alexi proceeded to read excerpts, and Hugo had to pull it from his hands, close it, and say, "Very nice. But the haunting?"

Alexi recalled that on the night in question, he was sipping his drink and listening to Michael Bublé sing softly, and just as Alexi was beginning to nod off, he heard footsteps. Or he thought he did. Claudia was sleeping. Maybe Dulce had awoken and had come downstairs for a glass of milk. And thinking that those footsteps belonged to his daughter, he read on, sipped more scotch, until, suddenly, he heard a voice that stirred his heart. *"Stirred?"* At first, Hugo thought that Alexi was about to discuss what it was like to be haunted by a past lover—the one who had gotten away. Nope! Alexi said that he looked up from his reading, just a glance, and what he saw made him spill some scotch. It was his brother, Alberto. He stood there in woolen pants and a silk shirt, tucked in. "He looked so young," Alexi said. Seeing his brother standing there, reaching for a handful of cherries, he said, *How can this be, Alberto? We haven't spoken in years.* But Alberto paid him no attention.

What struck Alexi as particularly odd was Alberto's outfit. That silk shirt. It looked so familiar, down to the large sweat stain on his back. "That's when I realized," Alexi said, "it was the same outfit that my brother had worn for the Christmas party we threw so many years ago. What a time! It was supposed to be our Annual Ramirez Christmas Eve Party. Those were the days." And here, Alexi digressed. He narrated the incident well into the fog of his happiest days. No amount of redirection or guidance could prevent him from discussing the kind of champagne they served at the party, the person they'd paid to decorate their condo, and so on. Eventually, Hugo had to put his pen and notepad down, grab Alexi's hands, and say, "Alexi! I think you're really losing focus here."

"Sorry. Sorry," he said, a big fat smile on his round face. He continued, noting that when he tried to communicate with Alberto, his brother walked away, right to the giant McMansion front doors, and he swung them both open. In came three of his old employees, back from the old traffic-ticket days. And seeing them walk in, he claimed to have jumped up from the couch and onto the ottoman. Hugo didn't believe him, but he wrote it down anyway. And from the ottoman, Alexi shouted his past employees' names: *Irma! Pedro! Ernesto!* He was so happy to see them again, but that wasn't all. The party was only now just beginning. Because in came Alexi's ex-girlfriend Sonita. In came Alexi's parents and other siblings, God bless them. In came all kinds of people, some he recognized and others he'd never seen in his life. Some whom he'd hired on when he switched to debt, some whom he'd been happy to say goodbye to. No matter who, seeing them had put Alexi in good spirits. In came a waiter dressed all in black and lugging crates of alcohol. In came a DJ and two women dressed like Christmas elves, there for caroling and a little extra. And a guy wheeling in a churro machine—what an extravagance. Alexi had forgotten about the churro machine. "Coño. How have I not called the churro guy to another party? They were so fresh." In came some dudes in guayaberas, each serious and holding an instrument case. In came the alligator hunter, old and practically shirtless. Alexi couldn't remember his name, but "Damn," he said, "those were our parties. One minute, you're chilling. Then, some super famous Cuban alligator hunter walks in."

Inside his home, the guests circulated among his things, opening bottles of champagne, or wine, or beer, or tequila, and Alexi, overwhelmed by this impromptu party, by the buzzing conversations, jumped off the ottoman and yelled, *Everybody! What's going on here?* To which they all responded with Christmas carols, and the exchanging of presents, and kisses under the mistletoe. That is, everyone was in such wonderful spirits, but they all ignored him. Nobody greeted him. Nobody kissed his cheek. Nobody wished him a Merry Christmas. Still, he was filled with joy.

Hugo could see it on Alexi's face, just in telling the story, how happy he was to see his friends. Well, subordinates, really—the people he'd employed. But Alexi must have thought them friends. That Christmas party that he and Alberto had hosted downtown. "What a time!" Alexi said. They'd leased a condo—a bachelor pad—on the penthouse floor of a building named after some Indigenous group. "Who knows who?" Alexi laughed. "Who remembers the losers?

"And then," Alexi said, looking around as if he were afraid Claudia would hear him, "somebody switched off Bublé and the DJ put on Spam Allstars, and then it was a party." With all those merry souls dancing about, Alexi must have felt the full weight of his nostalgia awaken in him. Because he told Hugo that being at the party made him wonder: *What if I'd never married Claudia?*

Sonita found him by the couch, put her hand on his waist, her arm around his neck, and said, *Alexi, I have missed you so much.* And they danced—she in a sequin dress, he in his dirty sleep shirt. He kept asking her, *How is this all possible?* She didn't answer, but she kissed him, and feeling that kiss, Alexi remarked that it felt as though they'd never broken up. How he regretted being shitty toward her during a time of need. In that vision, holding her in his hands, he was so nervous. He felt like a young schoolchild. Love. All he could say was that he felt so much love.

And he worried, furiously, that Claudia would descend the staircase and put an end to the whole damn party. "It was like I was in a dream, man. And I knew I was in it. And I didn't want it to end. Not ever."

With the room getting crowded, Alberto opened the sliding glass door, and he shouted, drink in hand, *Pa'rriba, pa'bajo, pal'centro,* and then, with a huge grin, *pal'piscina!* The party erupted into the backyard. Somebody turned on the pool lights, the multicolored fountain. Somebody switched on the speakers. Everyone was in pairs, dancing, and Alexi was there with Sonita, as if their whole lives were still ahead of them. "I'm still friends with her on Facebook," he told Hugo. "Want to see?" To which Hugo responded, "No. Go on, please. What happened next?"

Alexi was dancing with Sonita, and she was shaking her hips and really leaning into him, getting him nice and excited. He closed his eyes, reached to kiss her, but then something unexpected happened. He fell into the pool. No! He believed that he might have been pushed. He fell like a lead weight. All of the logic of this world made no sense to him, the way he fell—so hard and fast. Underwater, he could see more guests, more past employees, or were they? These were different-looking, not dolled up for a party, but like rocks, like pieces of slate and mineral, and these rock people, they surrounded him, and they took hold of him, "hands that felt like the fucking pavement." They held him underwater. Then they wrapped him in chains—long chains. Alexi grabbed his own wrists and his neck to indicate how the chains had bound him. "And I looked into their red little eyes. Just little balls of fire. How could that be? Underwater? I looked at them, and I pleaded with my eyes. I pleaded, *Let me go, please.* But it's like they weren't even people. Just rocks. Not even things." In the haunting, there was a moment when Alexi was able to get his head above water. He thinks he did it by kicking frantically and climbing atop the very creatures trying to drown him. When his head broke the surface, what he saw frightened him. Everyone he'd ever loved—they were all standing there at the pool's edge, but broken, ashen and turning to smoke, eyes like hot coals. They looked like broken boulders, like things that get loaded in trucks and then driven off to pave highways. These creatures were becoming more and more like stone. And who should come into the water to shove Alexi's face under? Alberto, the only one who hadn't been transformed. His beloved brother. He palmed Alexi's skull and said, *To hell*, and then, as he pushed him under, he, too, turned to rock. Alexi was drowning. But really drowning. He claimed that he couldn't breathe. He thought he'd die.

When he awoke at the pool's edge, struggling to catch his breath, Claudia was there holding him, soaked from having jumped into the pool herself to save his life. As he came to, she asked, "What the fuck were you thinking?" Dulce was standing by the pool, too, crying. That's when Alexi said that he stood and looked around and around and saw that there was nobody else there. Nobody! There were no chains either—like a nightmare. He didn't know what bothered him more—that his cherished friends and family were gone yet again, or that, in his vision, they'd tried to drown him.

Claudia pressed him for answers: "Really! What the fuck is happening, Alexi?" And he told her everything, except the stuff about Sonita. "She doesn't need to hear that, okay? That's between me and you, man to man." But he told her about seeing

Alberto and about the party. He told her how the whole living room and backyard had been a dance floor, how there'd been so much booze and broken bottles, and how these rock people had tried to drown him. He even mentioned the thing about it being a Christmas Eve party. But there was, of course, nobody there. Not a soul, and when he reiterated to Claudia that there'd really been a party, she sent Dulce up to her room, and she slapped Alexi across the face, hard, and said, "You listen good, okay? You're seeing a therapist."

"Fuck!" Alexi said, exasperated. "I just get the creeps whenever I think about that night. Enough of that. I mean, what's to say those rock things don't come for Dulce or Claudia, too?"

Hugo set the notepad down. The story reminded him of something Lourdes had once said, how even the stones smile in their sleep. Hugo gestured to the evil eye bracelets that he'd offered, but which were still on the sofa next to him. "You should be wearing those. You all should."

10

AS HE LISTENED to Alexi's story, Hugo was quite sure that the haunting was the result of something between remorse and watching *The Muppet Christmas Carol* one too many times. This had to be the case. Here was a grown man, a miser by all accounts, alluding to chains and ghosts. As far as Hugo could tell, Claudia was correct. What Alexi needed wasn't una limpieza—he needed to make some time to speak with a professional. He needed meds, too. And maybe he needed to stop reading Carlos Eire. That nostalgia stuff really rots the mind. But Hugo wasn't going to say any of that. He was there to do his job, to have his debt forgiven. He felt for the attorney, just a little.

Alexi must have sensed his ill humor and disbelief because he took Hugo by the arm, and he said, "I'm not making this up!" And he led him to other spaces in the home where manifestations had occurred. By that point, Hugo wasn't really paying attention anymore. He'd gotten what he needed, quite certain now that the law firm would play into whatever solution he proposed. He was touring the stairwell, holding back a yawn, when he did see something. It was a figure shrouded in white. It shuffled off when he noticed, and it spooked him good. It must have been Dulce, he thought. She was sneaking around to listen in, but even this awareness brought him no peace.

"You sensed something, didn't you?" Alexi asked.

Hugo shook his head.

"Just tell me. I want to know."

"It's nothing, really. It's late. That's all."

"No. You saw one of them, right? Should we go upstairs?" Alexi asked, but it wasn't a question. He put his hand on Hugo's back and guided him up one creak of a step at a time.

Already, Hugo sensed a shift in atmosphere. It was cooler, for starters, and he had this irrational fear growing in him that something would jump out and scare him, just like in the films: *Boom! Aaah!* Hugo wanted to leave, but how could he—with Alexi behind him, shoving him along?

Upstairs, there was a long hallway, and at the very end, a door slightly ajar. It felt like a trap. Hugo had seen enough scary movies with Meli to know: If there was a demon in that house, *that* door would be the bait. The best course of action would be to turn around and leave—to forget the deal and everything. But this was no scary movie! Or it wasn't until Alexi noticed the door, too. "Coño," he said. "Is that? God! Do you see that? I never use that room." His fear was infectious.

"Try to remain calm," Hugo said, as if to himself. "Tell me. What's the room used for?"

"That's just it. Nothing. Claudia wants to make it an exercise room. It's small."

"Well then, case closed. I'm sure it's nothing."

But Alexi insisted that Hugo lead the way, so he did, one short step at a time.

Hugo could feel the air in the hall grow colder. It reminded him of something; he wasn't sure what. Had someone left a window in the room open? There was nothing else to explain the cool earthy breeze washing over him. As he got closer yet, Alexi was nearly on top of him, hand gingerly on his waist. It felt so ridiculous—two grown men doing the conga in a dark hall, with no music or anything. More than the situation, Hugo did not like having Alexi's hands on his body.

Just when Hugo was prepared to march forward, the adjacent bedroom door swung open. A figure emerged, wrapped in a white shawl. Hugo turned to Alexi and embraced him, much in the way he used to turn toward Santi when they'd visit the spook barns at the farms. Alexi shouted, "¡Sálvame, Claudia!" The figure smacked them both, turned on the lights, and said, "What the fuck! You're going to wake Dulce." It was Claudia, of course, who must have gotten up when she'd heard Alexi and Hugo sneaking about. The men had a nice and very quiet laugh about the incident. And Hugo, in much better spirits, looked to the door ahead of him, now swaying. He entered the room.

Though the light was on in the hallway, the room was still dark. As Alexi had reported, it was completely empty. A single window opposite the door invited just a bit of moonlight in, and as Hugo had thought, the window was open. Cool air was flowing in—unseasonably cold for Miami, but nice. Hugo flipped on the lights. Now he could see that there were crayons littering the floor. Dulce must have snuck in to color. Immediately, Claudia remarked on Dulce's mess. Near the door, and scribbled all over the wall, was a series of Dulce's little drawings. They were sloppy things. Disfigured, hardly recognizable, but nice. How innocent, that a child can see a canvas in anything.

When they noticed, Claudia and Alexi flipped their shit, and as they bickered about the proper way to raise their daughter, Hugo knelt by the drawings, admiring them, wishing that he'd had such a problem to deal with. Following her drawings across the wall, he came across something unusual that she'd written. It was hard to make out the letters at first. The *M* looked like a really basic version of a bird, and the horizontal line of the *L* was as long as the vertical one. But then Hugo saw it. He really saw it. It was impossible. Dulce had written "MELI" on the wall. Below it, she'd drawn black flowers, and what looked, to Hugo at least, like a volcano overflowing with lava. "Did you draw this?" Hugo asked, turning to Dulce, as if she were there next to him. But Dulce wasn't in the room. And this unsettled Hugo even more because he could have sworn somebody else was.

～

THE BLACK FLOWERS disturbed Hugo. How could Dulce know? As Alexi and Claudia argued, Hugo saw a woman's dress flash before his eyes. It was a memory from one of those endlessly hot and humid nights in Hialeah. The evening rush had ended. A trickle of cars sliced past; the botanica's front door was open to try and steal the occasional breeze. He could hear, in the nearby mango tree, the neighborhood flock of white-winged parakeets chattering. In preparing to close, Hugo was restocking the shelves. The store was a sauna. His shirt draped over him, heavy. As he reached into a box for a handful of votives, someone tapped him on the shoulder and said, "My God, Hugo. I don't believe it. Is that really you?" He stood to face the stranger, and she kissed him on the cheek.

Hugo hadn't heard her walk into the store. He was startled, and he took a step back. "Hi! I don't mean to be rude, but do I know you from somewhere?" he asked, a votive in his hand.

"Hugo! From Hialeah High. Mrs. Spinoza's class. Don't you remember?"

He did remember then, but Jess had looked so different in high school. And high school was such a long time ago. He hadn't even thought of Mrs. Spinoza in over a decade. He smiled, hugged her. "Yes. Yes, Mrs. Spinoza's class. Jess, I remember you. Forgive me. Wow! How are you?"

"How am I? God, what a question! Do you work here, Hugo?" She looked so pretty in her short cotton dress. It was a white dress covered in black flowers, overly formal for such a visit.

"I do. Can I help you find something?"

At this, Jess smiled. She put her finger to her lips, said, "It's a little embarrassing."

"Nonsense," Hugo said, setting the votives down. "We don't judge anyone here."

Jess stood closer, her body lightly against his, and said, "You look good, Hugo."

He wanted to say that she looked good, too. He felt that he should take a step back, create some distance between their bodies. He felt that he should mention Meli. It was hot. The parakeets were chirping madly. The smell of sage was strong. Hugo muttered, "Thank you," and he made eye contact with her, but this only made him want to kiss her—her soft-looking lips, full, and the intensity of her eyes, her faintly glittering eye shadow. "So, you need something?"

"My fiancé turned out to be gay," she said. "I feel like, right now, there's so much negative energy around me. Do you feel it? I mean, my friend Susie says she feels it, but she's no santero."

"I do feel it," Hugo said.

Jess grabbed his hand. "No, really. Feel it." She pulled at his hand as if to put it over her heart. Hugo could no longer withstand his attraction. This would not end well, he realized. So, he stepped away, awkwardly, clumsily, bumping into a glass display case—the little artifacts wobbling back and forth, nearly tumbling over and crashing onto the floor. "You okay?" she asked.

"I have just the thing for you," he said, immediately retreating to the back of the store.

He emerged with three devotionals, a small beaded talisman, and a list of instructions. Rather than approaching her, he walked behind the counter as if to ring her up. Jess, who seemed disappointed, and who was clearly feeling rejected by Hugo, set her handbag on the counter and searched for her wallet. She paid with a credit card. Hugo explained what to do with the merchandise. When he was done, he handed her a receipt, and to smooth things over, he said, "I hope this works for you, Jess. You should come by the store again in a month and let me know."

"I will," she said. She tapped the counter with her long nails. "See you in a month."

Only, when Hugo finally closed the store thirty minutes later, Jess was outside, still waiting around. "Hey there," she said, pushing herself off a newspaper stand and approaching him.

"Hey. It's you."

"I just wanted to apologize. Things got a little weird in there. I didn't mean for that."

"Weird?" Hugo said. "No. It's just nice to see you again."

"You know," she said, "I could use some help setting up those candles."

"You want me to help?"

"Yeah, it's a lot of steps, and I'm new to this. And I *really* want it to work, you know?"

"Well, I'm sure we could set up a time. How's your week looking?"

"Hugo, I live like two blocks away. Right now is fine by me."

So, they walked to her place, which was not two blocks away. It was more like five. At Jess's home, after setting up the candles, they drank sangria, listened to the radio. Hugo texted Meli to let her know that he'd be running late. When he followed up by telling Jess that he had to leave, she sidled up beside him, put her hand on his thigh. She said, "I've been thinking about you so much. And now you're here! Did you know that in high school, I had such a crush on you? Big time."

She leaned in and kissed him, sliding her hand to his crotch. "No," he said. "I didn't."

"Tell me," she said. "Did you ever have a crush on me?"

He wasn't sure. God! When he met Jess, he'd just moved to Miami. He'd just enrolled at Hialeah High. Back then, everything was so new. Did he have a crush on her? He didn't answer.

Now, in her living room, he didn't protest. Something had been set in motion, and he wasn't sure he had the will to stop it. When the act was done—after she led him to her bedroom, and after they made love in a room of flickering spiritual candles—he didn't acknowledge any of it. He merely grabbed Jess's dress from the floor and put it on her bed. Then he dressed, frantically, and, after washing his face, said, "I have to go."

"Don't be like that. You can stay if you like," she said. "It's okay with me."

"I have a wife, Jess. I think I really do need to leave now."

"Wait! You're married?"

As Hugo prepared to walk out, Jess took one of the devotionals he'd sold her, all warm and pooling with melted wax, and she threw it at him. The wax burned his arm. The candle rolled along the floor, making a mess and snuffing the flame. "Does anything at your botanica actually work?"

"I don't know," Hugo said, wincing. "It works for some people. I don't believe it myself."

"You should've told me you were married. Fuck my life!"

"I'm sorry," Hugo said, picking up the devotional. "I'm really sorry."

"Leave it! Get the fuck out of here," she said.

Hugo sipped the last of his sangria and took one last look at Jess; then he left. On the walk back to the botanica, he felt sick. Why had he acted this way? Every scratch Jess had inflicted on him—the burn of the wax—was evidence of his infidelity. Worse, the guilt festered inside him.

Later, when he got home and showered and climbed into bed, he thought Meli would smell it on him for sure. He thought she'd